UNDERWATER

Other books by the author:

Bailey
Trespass
Rematch
Family Money

UNDERWATER

JOAN HAWKINS

Landon Books

First Published by
GP Putnam, Books, New York, 1974

2nd Print Edition by
Landon Books, New York, 2014
Electronic edition published by 451 Editions, 2022

www..joanhawkins.net

ISBN 978-0-9837348-5-7

Book and cover design by www.Cyberscribe.ie

UNDERWATER

1

The two women packed away clothes in the hot New York house. There had been a death there two days before. Costumed in her dead mother's ancient fox fur piece and black felt hat, Elizabeth Graves presented herself to her cousin, who'd left the boxes on the floor and stretched out for a moment on the bed.

She tipped the brim dramatically over her eyes and pitched up her chin. "Mother was a flapper, Kate! Can you believe that?" She came over to the bed and looked down at her cousin with smoldering eyes. She thrust out her hip and said in a voice that was quite unnerving:

"Stay out of my pants, you son of a bitch! I'm a lady."

Three years the elder, Elizabeth had introduced Kate to all the bold and dashing women movie stars of the past two decades. She was dark and tall with a low voice and Kate was used to her quick parodies. Kate felt her neck and face begin to burn.

Elizabeth laughed delightedly and rubbed her cousin's hair.

"Kate Stevens, you're blushing! How funny!"

Elizabeth turned and looked at herself in the mirror over the bureau. Her denim overalls hung loosely from her shoulders, obscuring her strong figure. Perched on her shoulder, the little fox faces stared briskly back at Kate, bouncing suddenly as Elizabeth slammed her fist down on the bureau top.

"Damn you, Mother!" She pulled off the black hat and slapped it against her leg; the dust exploded violently in the bright air.

"She didn't lift a finger for herself. She could have come to me in the summers. She could have left him permanently – God, I begged her to live with me. But she wouldn't budge!"

The sound of faint barking was heard above their heads. Elizabeth stared at the ceiling, above which her sick, senile old father existed, attended by nurses from morning to night. He had a gift for imitating dogs and it had become an obsession. While at times he would yip and yap agreeably enough, more often he would persecute the inhabitants of the house with long bursts of demanding, spiteful barking.

"Shut up, you whiney old fuck!" Elizabeth ripped the fur piece from her neck and tore off the dry, dusty little fox heads, flinging them back into the closet, with its rows of dark, bulky clothing.

"He barked her crazy – he barked her to death."

Kate rose from the bed and hobbled to her cousin, a pair of fifty-year-old silver pumps swimming on her feet. The purple beaded skirt of the flapper's dress that Elizabeth had dug from the back of her mother's closet and enticed Kate to put on oscillated crazily across her thighs at each step. She put her arms around her cousin's waist and pressed her head against her back.

"I'm so sorry," she murmured, then drew abruptly

away as she felt Elizabeth stiffen. The sympathy that had launched her from the bed had also launched her mind from what Kate referred to since leaving the hospital as "my ambiguous bosom." Elizabeth, who had not yet seen her carved-away breast, had just registered the single pressure of Kate's bosom on her horrified back.

"Those shoes, that dress," Elizabeth laughed gaily and reached for the brush on the bureau top. "You look smashing!"

Kate stood like a statue while Elizabeth brushed the hair off her hot brow and cheeks, smoothing it behind her ears and down her back. The black felt hat arched flamboyantly in the air between Elizabeth's hands and settled on Kate's head. Because Elizabeth was taller, darker, fiercer than she, Kate had always adored her cousin, doting on her looks and style to the direct disparagement of her smaller, milder self. She now shivered violently as Elizabeth's adjusting hands left the brim of the hat and closed softly on her bare neck.

"Katey Edwards," she called in a rough, teasing voice. The challenge of her maiden name drew Kate's shy gaze from beneath the dusty brim and she met the swift, lustful sweep of her cousin's eyes.

Bumping Kate saucily with her hips, Elizabeth sang: "I wish I could shimmy like my cousin Kate."

Before Kate could respond, her mouth dropping open in the effort, Elizabeth confronted their images in the mirror with a mean smile. "Well, it beats masturbation!"

She whirled round and kicked over a box that Kate had laboriously filled with the contents of her aunt's bureau, then stooping, flung them back.

Kate felt her cousin's subtle barb and it was her turn to stiffen.

"Get that obscene thing off, will you?" Kate drifted dumbly to the bathroom.

"I'm getting out of here," Elizabeth fumed. "It's too hot to live!"

Loping down the dark stairs, then shuffling about the kitchen while Elizabeth directed the caterers about the trays and glasses to be used, then pulling back up to the top of the house, where the nurse was told what suit the old man was to wear, Kate waited in vain for her indignant silence to be noted. How dare Elizabeth react as if she had been criticized? It was her old way of assuming that Kate's marriage to Harry Stevens had stuffed her sexual imagination into a rock-weighted bag that sank deeper and deeper into conventional gloom. If her cousin had given her a chance to speak, she would have found Kate exhilarated by the suggestion of lesbianism.

At last seated in her cousin's bedroom, Kate followed with accusing eyes as Elizabeth took off her overalls and sneakers and, in a man's blue shirt and white wool socks, walked up and down the small, stark room, telephoning.

It upset the minister that the service should be given in a funeral home and not in the chapel of the church that Mrs. Graves had particularly loved. Kate half-listened while Elizabeth described to the minister her father's petulance on the subject of his wife's interment. He was a taxpayer, after all, lived all his life in New York, why shouldn't the state assume the funeral expenses? As for buying a coffin, if it hadn't been against the law to bury the dead awash in their own juices and wrapped around in a plastic bag – the director of the funeral home had set her father straight on that – her mother would be laid out right this minute like a chicken in the supermarket. Elizabeth winked at Kate as she hung up.

Kate tipped back in the desk chair, floating Elizabeth on the top of her mind as though it were a smooth, watery surface. Her motions took familiar and exciting shape, that of yellow chrysanthemums in lavish graceful bunches. Her cousin was now on the phone to the florist to be sure that her mother's favorite autumn flower – there was no point in substitution – had been sent out to the funeral home.

Kate daydreamed as she watched, followed, waited for her cousin. As long as Kate could remember, it had been Elizabeth's response to laugh at her good-humored vagueness and to accuse her of complying with her plans for the sake of pleasing her. Good God, she'd follow her into the East River in the middle of winter, she'd say. Then when the younger girl invariably responded that whatever Elizabeth wanted to do, wherever she wanted to go, never failed to strike Kate as the exact target of her desire, Elizabeth would warm Kate with a look of tender incredulity

Kate's flowered silk dress spread over the foot of Elizabeth's bed; her glossy green sandals were set neatly on the rug below. The deodorant, the powder, and lipstick that she'd use to prepare herself for her aunt's service were all neatly arranged in the medicine chest in Elizabeth's bathroom. The two young women had grown up together, passing fluidly between the two New York houses, each one feeling that the other's was her second home. They were related through their mothers, who, although aloof and incurious in their day-to-day contact, believed in loyalty in the political way of large and wealthy families.

Kate and Elizabeth believed in intimacy.

That her cousin was dashing, original, and utterly sensible in what she wore and read and advocated was as obvious to Kate as the great dread that they carried between them like a huge black banner. Namely, that if they didn't struggle from the current that had claimed their mothers, they would end up like them, slowly drowning, day to day.

The previous autumn, however, when Kate lay in the hospital, the light and humorous quality of their intimacy had ceased. It was displaced by the hard waves of Elizabeth's disapproval of Kate's now-resistant spirit. So Kate had not wanted to be a lawyer anymore? Just walked away from a job so intensely coveted by women less fortunate in parental connections than she? Because taking into account her father and, of course, her brains, Kate might well become one of the few woman partners in a Wall Street firm.

The solid pine chair creaked under her as Kate watched Elizabeth dial yet another call, to Kate's husband this time, at the law school where he and Elizabeth both taught.

That morning Harry Stevens had been about to put on a bright blue shirt and yellow tie when Kate reminded him of the funeral. Harry taught constitutional law and a few months before had been made assistant dean in charge of admissions, a choice of some political significance, for Harry was a dramatic and liberal presence in the City

Law School. The students overwhelmingly favored him while the faculty, the older ones in particular, thought him suspiciously opportunistic.

To Kate he was a solid, warm wall behind which she lusted in the night.

Elizabeth was his assistant, both in teaching and political strategy. Kate's marriage had initially linked her cousin to Harry Stevens; their intense impatience with the state of the world soon stimulated a warm friendship, and Harry had pressed hard and successfully to have her hired as an associate professor. For months they'd worked on proposals of reform and Elizabeth would have been by his side at the faculty meeting that very afternoon had it not been that her mother was to be buried.

Heartily, seriously, Elizabeth wished Harry luck, then pitched her head forward in a heavy, unsubtle way as Harry's laughter carried past her head to Kate. It was the same manner that had driven Kate half mad during Elizabeth's hospital calls the year before. Elizabeth loomed her will over Kate's bed and Kate felt the weight of it on her wounded chest as though it were a boulder.

She was not able to tell Elizabeth that she was no longer just herself, that she was, in fact, sharing space with a figment of her imagination: a girl she had named Valery St. John, who'd swum to the top of her consciousness in college and commanded all the stories Kate had written. How could she explain? Elizabeth's strong moral brow prevented her from saying that she'd ditched her imagination too often before, allowing its implications to bear down her courage and bow her finally to the will of her father.

He'd persuaded her to go to law school, then talked her into working in the firm where he'd begun fifteen years before. She'd married, had a baby, a well-loved girl, called Cam.

Her stitches pulled cruelly in her demand for her cousin's respect. Even her father had apologized for the work Kate had been hired to do, but not seriously, for what you did was not the point if, when doing it, you excelled above all others. Born beyond social or financial ambitions, Kate could not see the point of remaining an intellectual mercenary.

"But women have to fight!" Saliva glittered in the corners of Elizabeth's earnest mouth when she said it. "They have to take advantage of opportunities, grow confident, gain power, and slowly, bit by bit, lever all women into the sun!"

"Valery St. John!" Kate had shouted with stinging eyes.

"And who," Elizabeth incuriously wondered, "is she?"

She was Kate's fictional girl. A girl who drove a yellow convertible, kept gin in the dashboard, and climbed up the gutters of the snug dormitories and into the beds of exciting women.

But Elizabeth had read enough fiction. Fiction, said her puritanical eyes, was for people who couldn't get out of bed. Then the nipple on Kate's excavated breast began to coldly, coldly feel and her arm came up from her side to fasten over the right side of her chest, her fingers catching the knob of bone at the end of the shoulder. Elizabeth left her, but that look did not.

16

Kate returned to the room with a bang, as Elizabeth, still on the telephone, pointed to the clock on the bedside table and then to the bathroom door. The service for her aunt was not until the end of the afternoon, but Elizabeth had promised to take Kate early to the funeral home, because she had asked to see her aunt privately, to say goodbye.

The steam from the hot shower softened the impact of the close, glossy white bathroom walls. The mirrored door of the medicine chest held her image and she greeted it, through the comfortable air, with a raised arm and a smile.

"Hi ya, kid. Doing all right?"

She gathered her thick, goldish hair in her right fist, then turned, her practiced sideways glance discovering the shorn profile and flat chest of a handsome youth. If she did say so herself. The broad red crescent of scar was revealed only if she raised her right arm. Its calamitous hue was guaranteed to fade. So said the family doctor when he'd stood by her hospital bed and assured her that the best cancer man in the city had done one hell of a job. But he'd neglected to tell her that in the cleaned-out spaces an idea had lodged. Had ballooned!

Since college sternly ignored, Valery St. John now fiercely filled the young woman's wounded chest.

Kate let go of her hair and stood full face to the hospitable glass square. In the mild interval of space, the overhead light discovered the surprising off-and-on quality of her chest by the narrow, curved shadow it poured over the left breast.

It was now well past a year since the firm had granted Kate Stevens a leave of absence – even the operation had drifted beyond the lee of consideration – and still the young woman who stared with such fascination at her redesigned trunk had not returned to the practice of law.

Her father, her employer for five years and now a newly appointed judge, was contemptuous of her when sober; with gin, rotten rude.

In the bright, hot bathroom, the voice of her cousin on the telephone coming through the door, Kate Stevens rotated her torso in front of the cloudy mirror. Huge-eyed, faintly smiling, she twisted herself from gender to gender, her hand pressing her flat chest, then closing in amazement on the flesh of her small breast.

The cold, explicit way that Elizabeth had said the word "masturbate" did not in the least remind Kate of the subtle feeling of her hand as it translated images to sensation.

She stood on tiptoe, her legs braced against the sink. The sight of her hand and the bright, curling hair beneath assured her. Hers were pleasuring, interpretive, sportive fingers, not the members of a masturbatory club.

Oh, no!

The knob turned imperiously and Kate reached wildly for a towel. She barely had time to register Elizabeth's expression, when she was alone again. Her hand closed on a white towel that she no longer needed but pressed almost compulsively to her flesh, which had shown itself in the moment of Elizabeth's survey to be in a state of appalling mutilation.

Elizabeth's low, teasing voice at the door frightened her. "Hurry, downstairs, now, I'll be waiting for you."

Kate ran warm water over her hand while she brushed

her teeth. As she powdered away the gleam on her cheeks and forehead, she listened desperately for the sound of Harry's voice inside her head, telling her that Elizabeth was just Elizabeth.

Of course, there would be a certain shyness and tension, even fear, in seeing Kate's chest for the first time after her operation. But the look that had made her want to run away – that look had been supplied by Kate herself, by her puritanical habit of self-criticism. It had gotten out of hand with her and had grown through the years into a monstrous enemy that she harbored within her gates.

She combed her hair, then stepped out into the empty room, where she hurriedly dressed.

2

The neat, green toes of Kate's sandals led her down the dark staircase and out into the street, the flowered hem of her short, silk dress cresting at the edge of her vision. She waited for Elizabeth in the tiny courtyard before the house. She leaned against the gatepost and brooded.

Night after night her self-given pleasure passed like fast waves over the surface of her desire, leaving it solid and cold. She wished that she might fold herself together like the leaves of a book, oh, peace in our times.

The cook rapped on the window with a spoon, then leaned and shouted through the crack that Elizabeth had gone not a minute before.

Kate hung onto the gatepost and traced the numbers stuck in the wood. Number twelve. Her fingers traced the hot, bright curves of metal while she waded to the waist in shadow. An artery had blown in her aunt's head. Her uncle was yapping high inside the house. Barks like darts.

The pool of shadow thrown by the house across the street slid up her hand, quenching the blue glow of her wedding ring. She must push off from this post. The funeral home was very near and Elizabeth was waiting, but the proven impossibility of fucking her own mind was stalling her with gloom.

"Off this track" – she swung open the gate – "your aunt is dead."

Walking, the young woman beamed her eyes in a slow circle. Narrow house fronts flashed by, some near, some far, here with sun, there without. A street like the street where Kate's parents lived, but way downtown, Washington Square Park nearby, the Village and Sixth Avenue opening brightly at its end. Kate hurried, the violent curb smells of urine and dog shit transforming her guilt to fury. Surely death ought to cool her down.

Valery St. John had legs like steel bands sheathed in tight blue denim. Her belts were wide but not thick. She had charm in her voice, was buoyant and graceful, funny and fierce.

Across the street, on top of a warehouse, a snowy-haired, stately man was painted, seated at a desk. He eyeballed a strenuous expression of solicitude. Kate looked sternly back, read aloud the black letters of his message. "A funeral should never cost more than a family can afford." The head of a black arrow hooked round the side of the building.

Mr. Graves was rich enough to afford eccentricity. He hated to part with a penny. Nearly fifty when his second wife burdened his irritable lust with consequence, he'd received Elizabeth as a guest, who'd one day be leaving, but who, in the meantime, required the top floor of his house and an outrageously large portion of his inherited income. To lay out money for his wife after her departure made him bark like a mad dog.

The funeral home had a purple door. Kate pushed against the polished handle and stepped onto a soft carpet, holding her breath. The juices of the dead were drained off in such places, making room for the preserving fluid. She

21

saw Elizabeth pass by a doorway at the end of the room, carting a folding chair. Her bangs were swept to one side and the accepted loneliness expressed by her high, white brow made Kate walk straight toward her, her fast sliding soles sparkling in the thick rug. She turned suddenly at a harsh tapping of glass. An irascible female voice came amplified from a glass cubicle beside the front door.

Bending to a cluster of holes in the glass, Kate looked with wonder at a woman's face wrathfully established beneath a huge dome of orange hair.

"I'm here for the service," Kate explained.

"Well, you have one hell of a nerve, walking straight past, as if you owned the place! I am the receptionist and not some goddamned parrot to breeze by."

Elizabeth, walking moodily in a beige cotton dress, came down the hall. Always wore a scoop neck and long sleeves, always looked noble and calmly challenging from under her thick bangs.

Old-fashioned in the fullness of her neck and serene breadth of her shoulders, she spoke humbly through the holes to the furious female behind glass, saying she'd found just a bit too much lipstick on her mother's face and a touch more rouge than her old father was accustomed to seeing.

"My father is so old and cranky, would you mind if I used a bit of your cold cream? There's no time to go out to a drugstore."

The woman looked irritably at Kate, who held up her empty hands and politely smiled.

"All the dead are got up like that," complained the voice as Elizabeth walked away with the cream. It was artistic – to make them look alive.

Kate stepped just inside the door, then leaned against the frame. The shape and size of the space were familiar, as was the way the simple pine coffin divided it. Her hospital room, yes, the bed jutting from the wall with the tables on either side, but here, marble pedestals to go with the imperial purple walls.

How could the family all fit? Kate asked.

Elizabeth smelled of lemons and picked a roll of yellow toilet paper off a pedestal, whose partner across the coffin lid carried yellow chrysanthemums that drooped in the thick, hot air.

Due to the expense of advertising a death in the newspaper, and the not-insignificant cost of long distance phone calls, the family, outside of Kate's mother, had not been notified and so could not possibly threaten the minuscule space rented out for the service.

"Aunt Mary, Uncle David, you, Harry, Father, and myself, plus the minister, who I hope is very thin. That makes seven." Elizabeth looked wryly around the tiny space. "Perfectly swell, if the air holds out."

Concentrating on the various forms and textures of yellow, Kate stepped up to the coffin. Elizabeth motioned her around the other side, where the raised lid blocked a view of the interior.

"Incredible as it may seem, Mother dear, they've got you all painted up like a whore."

Elizabeth's mouth drew down at the corners as her hand, bearing yellow toilet paper and a gob of cold cream, ducked behind the coffin lid.

"Kate has come to pay her respects and I can't have her see you like this. Not that you shouldn't have gone a

23

touch down this road. A few affairs would have jazzed up the old, gray in and out."

Her cousin flashed a broad grin across the coffin lid. "Ludicrous, eh? Who'd want this banged-up, bruised old wreck!"

"I – " Kate tried to speak.

Elizabeth glared. "I what?"

Kate held hard to the edge of the coffin and tried to breathe from the bottom of her lungs.

"Now I can see that bruise on her forehead, she looks like her old self, whom she never lifted a finger for, I might add." She rapped her knuckles against the coffin side. "Want to look now?" Elizabeth stepped back, her hands full of greasy paper. She smiled gently at Kate. "She's not nearly as white as you are."

Elizabeth squeezed her shoulder as Kate looked in, not at the face, but at the hands holding each other and the rings, which had never been still in Kate's sight before, the settings spun round by nervous fingers as her aunt rustled, rushed about, crashed. Kate's eyes climbed up the glossy black buttons on her aunt's chest. She leaped back, the blind, heavy face the merest flash in her mind.

"I won't!" she shouted at Elizabeth.

"Won't?" Elizabeth stepped up against Kate, her mean, smiling face bearing down. "You won't?"

Kate jabbed her clenched fist at the coffin. "I won't be like that! No!"

Elizabeth leaned from the door of the funeral home, calling after her. Kate turned, waved, and ran on.

The service was in twenty minutes but there was a shop she knew on Eighth Street and some clothes she had to buy.

She ran for blocks. On the curb, waiting for cars to pass, she plucked the hem of her dress from between her legs.

The owner of the shop, whom Kate slightly knew, looked her humorously up and down.

"In freak weather like this, it's walk, not run. Didn't you know?" She handed Kate a towel. "Dry yourself off while I get the jeans." She was back in a whiz, a pair of size ten Levi's dangling from her hand.

"Now, you want some sort of navy blue shirt, preferably with a V-neck and long sleeves." She studied Kate's hips. "A brown leather belt, wide but not thick, and whatever size seven sandals or informal shoes are in stock."

The owner wrapped Kate's dress and green shoes in tissue paper and put them in a box.

"If you run in that shirt" – she opened the shop door, patting Kate's tightly sheathed bottom as it passed – "it will dissolve."

On the corner of Sixth Avenue and Eighth Street, Kate Stevens, dressed as Valery St. John, dropped her neatly boxed old clothes into the trash can. On the next block she saw a lithe transvestite, tall and lean, unfurling the dress, the tissue paper sailing beneath the wheels of the huge, thundering trucks, the green shoes perched on one shoulder while he seriously regarded his find. He strode off with a triumphant flap and swirl of Kate Stevens' flowered skirt.

Valery hurled open the door of the funeral joint, strode past the woman in her box of glass and acknowledged the amplified curses and flaming hair, with a republican nod and wave. Viewed from any other point of view but their own, were they not sisters?

Another door to open, but respectfully. From behind the thin wood came the firm, tones of "Yea, though I walk through the valley of the shadow of death, I will fear no evil."

The girl's blindly intrepid entrance landed her foot on her father's shiny, black shoe.

"For thou art with me," she hopefully joined in.

Her father's hand closed meanly over the wrist that she'd so admired in her walk from the Eighth Street shop, its repeated flash of buoyant blue.

"Amen," he threatened.

Across her father's hard-breathing chest, her mother glanced at her with complete disinterest, then resettled her eyes on the coffin. During the prayers that followed, she slid her handbag up to her elbow, felt the strap on her wrist again, and, groaning, slid it back. It was the discontented, restless sound she made at home while reading on the couch or struggling with an ice tray or going to the phone. It was a private, undirected, perhaps unregistered complaint that, heard in this public place, filled Valery with pity and dread.

Mr. Graves shuffled past on Elizabeth's arm, his head pitched forward, his lips trembling at his stiff tread. Her father glared at his back. "Decadent old fool," he exploded.

Outside the funeral home Harry Stevens came loping up. He hadn't counted on the evening traffic and the scarcity of cabs. He helped Mr. Graves into the limousine, then stood for a moment with Elizabeth, talking intensely. That morning, regretfully dressed in charcoal gray, his bright shirt and tie thrown down on the bed, he'd wondered, half-seriously, if he'd have the nerve to defend his reforms when shorn of his colors.

Judge Edwards' official car swept in behind the hired limousine.

"Come on," his wife commanded and pitched out of his grasp. Mary Edwards was just sixty, yet her long, stiff legs provided such an insecure base that on the street the judge never left her side. Now, springing to stabilize her, he let go of his daughter, who walked rapidly away.

Harry helped Elizabeth in beside her father, then responded blandly to the judge's signal and slipped by him at the door to sit beside his mother-in-law.

Valery drew back from the curb as the judge leaned out the door of the slowly cruising car. "I'll walk," she told her father.

"I'll walk with Kate" said Harry, coming slowly into the situation, then peered incredulously down at the thick, pin-striped arm that blocked his passage.

Her father shook his finger through the window.

"You are not to appear at the funeral supper dressed in jeans or you'll be punished."

"What are you going to do, lock her up?" his wife asked satirically.

"Oh, damn," cried the judge and the car sped. Trapped between her parents, Harry hooked around. She waved at his astonished face.

Harry was trapped. He was physically too big to lightly forgive his father-in-law's bullying will but so slowly did he swim up to the moment that the car would be emptied, the house entered, the situation melted beneath him before he could take hold.

This amiable, unflinching openness, so different from Kate's tart response to the present, and the fact that her father had arranged a dinner to introduce them, had caused Kate to lump his temperament and his mind and call him stupid. That he was an ex-football player from the South fortified her eager prejudice against her father's ardent endorsement of his intellect. He badly wanted Harry to join his firm, but when it became clear that Harry wanted to teach, he introduced him to one of his long-time friends, the dean, as he put it, of "the country's best second-rate law school." Harry crested under bright skies there from the very beginning.

His liberal reputation was a magnet to Elizabeth, who'd burst from law school, longing for a fight. Right from the beginning they were ardent allies, praising to the skies each other's intellectuality and generous social impulses. But Elizabeth, in a gray and cautious system, had the ballast and excitement of her feminine pride, while Prince Harry was a drunk. He drank because he loathed the swarm of dry men, who crouched behind closed doors, word-knitting their careers. Also, he drank, and so did Kate, because their fondness for each other and day-to-day intimacy made their sex life inexplicably painful.

Valery St. John confidently turned away from the avenue, introducing to her crisp, angular stride the motion of her hips. She sailed down steps. A glass chandelier lit the narrow front hall. Steep stairs lay directly before her. She put her foot on the black carpet and climbed. A burst of barking pressed her back into the curve of stairs, her heart fuming, yet sinking at the close-following sound of her father's rich, cordial voice. Of course, he would have a drink and his handsome son-in-law would have one too.

Dragging her hand on the banister, Kate walked to the front of the house, where the two drawing rooms opened on either side of the hall. The slightly larger room was half filled with a grand piano covered with a white cloth, glasses and bottles of appallingly cheap booze. After an evening there, Kate's mother would inevitably say that if she shot herself before the day was out, it was entirely the fault of her sister, who evidently could not deter her husband from serving straight poison to her own family. Why was it so difficult to understand that the horrifying physical effects did not result from the quantity of booze drunk, which was admittedly great, but from the fact that the stuff had been distilled five minutes ago?

Drinking, drunkish, sighing, crying, Mary Edwards proclaimed bad whiskey to be the cause of her younger sister's death; the rotten raw stuff had cut through her veins and arteries like acid. Damn her skinflint husband.

Kate's father, the judge, felt grief was sludge to be burned out fast. That thought swerved her into the smaller room. She pushed through the French doors at the end of the room and stood on the balcony. At the back of the garden, a brick wall, handsome in the daylight, slept. A bar of orange light suddenly existed there as the dining room door opened and the minister came out into the garden. He shut the door behind him and walked toward the dark wall.

Valery stepped reluctantly back into the room, then stopped and hung onto the door. Someone was reading on the couch, reading there in black, swirling trousers and big black boots. The small china lamp was pulled to the edge of the table, looking like a captured bunny. A large, capable hand tipped up the shade and held it; a drink balanced on a steady knee.

A burst of barking came from the room across the way, abruptly doused by the judge's commanding voice. Whenever Elizabeth's father looked into the judge's face, he saw the twin reflection of a gibbering old fool.

The long, strong fingers plowed again and again through short, dark curls, flicked over a page, lifted a glass. Must be one of Elizabeth's radical pals, but what was he reading? The young woman glanced timidly into the reader's lap as she passed and was startled to read *Pride and Prejudice* at the top of the page. At her back a light, teasing voice said:

"Why are you alone? Why am I? Isn't there supposed to be a party?"

"Well, not exactly!" Kate said.

A mocking flash of green eyes under penciled brows.

"What's your name, darling?"

Kate straightened, quietly said: "Valery St. John."

The woman on the couch lifted her glass, coolly cocked her penciled brows, and smiled.

"Cheers."

Valery idled in the hallway between the two rooms. Her father stood with Harry within the curve of the piano top, the quiet black line tolerant of the professor's look of rough wood, and the judge, smooth and shiny like a polished stone.

In the corner of the narrow doorway, she could see the end of the couch, round which peeped her mother's foot, a black pump jiggling from her toes.

Elizabeth came around the stairs and gazed upon her cousin with a salty little smile.

"You look good. Not that I understand."

Valery hugged her hard. "There's the most amazing person" – she pointed across Elizabeth's stomach to the quiet drawing room – "she's reading Jane Austen in big, black boots."

As Valery spoke, a dark figure loomed from the narrow doorway, a black Spanish hat pushed back on her curls.

"I'm splitting!" She yawned. Elizabeth stepped in front of her and said fiercely,

"You promised, Margo!"

"I did come! I've sat in there for an hour ... ah, shit." She turned back into the room, "At least get me another drink!"

Elizabeth glided back to Kate and pressed her arm with averted eyes.

"In five minutes or so would you bring a martini across to her? I've got to go down to the kitchen." She smiled at Harry, who waved to her over the judge's shoulder. "Poor guy, he got smashed today."

"Was that why he missed the service?"

"I gather." Elizabeth gazed into the festive precinct.

"Isn't it interesting that the two men in your life are so different." She smiled charmingly. "I mean your father is such a shit."

"Katie!" Harry threw out his long arm, snagging her on her way to the couch, where her mother sat.

He peered gaily over the smudged steel-rimmed glasses that sat crookedly on his face.

"You look marvelous!"

"Ah, Christ!" the judge cried. "Don't encourage her!" Harry smiled mildly at his father-in-law.

"She looks really good in jeans."

Stepping back as if to get a clarifying view of this large young man, the judge declared that even a country boy, like Harry, who had to be thrown on his back to get his shoes on, knew enough to wear his best suit to a funeral.

He looked coldly at his daughter. "You're too old for stunts. You look like your own teenage daughter."

"When I was a teenager, I was ancient!"

The distress in her voice softened her father's eyes and voice, but his strong arm clamped around her waist. His chest was like steel beneath the soft wool of his suit.

"When you were a teenager you were terrific. You've always been terrific – my god, Harry, this gal has a finer legal mind than I do. She was one of the best associates the firm has had in years and just when she gets within shooting range of a partnership, she up and quits."

Kate stared into her father's tough, attractive face, feeling the hard waves of his bullying will against her hot skin. In terms of success he'd moved himself to countries far from the place of his birth; he would move her too if she'd let him. He glared at her again, his arm tightening.

"She was working on the most important case – "

"I hated working on that damned anti-trust case," Kate said in a small, high voice. "I wanted to go to court."

"Work is work," Judge Edwards snapped. "You could have been a partner by now, one of the handful of women partners on Wall Street, but you have to sit at home being sensitive, feeling sorry for yourself."

She pushed against his ribs. "I was so bored!"

"Join the human race," he sneered.

A pale, stark laugh flew out of her. "I intend to."

He loosened his grip and looked at her chest. "Ah, Katie!" The pressure of her one breast against his hard body, the egotism of his assumption that shorn of her womanly flesh she would not dare go forth to battle, made her shout.

"I was letting you get to me! No more!"

The judge contracted and cooled, became again the hard, polished stone with which Kate could deal, unflooded by grief and regret. Once she had been his girl flying down his tracks but something had happened. The rush of whatever it was she hooked to the skillful excavation of her ambiguous bosom. The hooking was arbitrary and didn't interest her. What did was the invasion, that fictional girl now bursting her insides with her hurting growth.

Her father's charming smile froze in the bitter distance between them. "Your loud voice is unbecoming for the wife of a southern gentleman."

"Harry's not a gentleman, he hates 'em."

"Well, he looks like a gentleman. The fact that he's trying to turn a distinguished school of law into a loathsome social service implies a certain aristocratic woolly-headedness." The judge's caustically fond tone made Harry smile.

"He behaves like one and by god, he's certainly married like one."

"My God, sir."

The judge's imperious hand stopped him dead. Harry

looked at the broad palm as if wondering wherein lay its power.

"Don't be a goddamned fool! You've got the deanship in the palm of your hand and you're going to lose it if you can't leave well enough alone."

The judge watched the electrical effect of his words with satisfaction.

"Dean Bender was at the opera last night and we had a rather interesting talk about you." He clapped Harry on the shoulder. "He's definitely decided to step down. His health is bad and he doesn't feel he can cope with all the political unrest."

"He's been mentally dead for three decades," Kate said, grinning at Harry. "Right?"

Judge Edwards moved in front of her, his broad body blocking everything of Harry but his still, intense face.

"He feels a younger man should take his place and the board of trustees agrees with him. He's very impressed with the way you've advocated for the inclusion of African American students on the school's recruitment program. He thinks it shows great executive talent but what he wanted to get from me was an insight into your commitment to it."

"He knows that!" Harry's humorous and fatalistic look mastered the excitement that had momentarily glazed his face.

"Knows what?"

"I talked Dean Bender into this new program, then I travelled round to the colleges and spoke to young African American students, inviting them to enroll with us. But now I'm talking my head off trying to keep them

34

at the school, because they're having a harder time than they expected."

"Well, that's simple," the judge said with a shrug. "You can just shut up."

"Why?"

"Can't you see that you've made a mistake? They're not up to the work."

"I don't agree. The real reason some of my colleagues want to go back on the inclusion program is that they've suddenly had to admit that our new black students are well able for the work. They're smart, cool, politically sophisticated kids."

"Dean Bender thinks that a Trojan horse has been slipped inside his gates. How did he put it? 'I've tuned in late, but I've tuned in clear.'"

"He couldn't be more wrong. He's missing the boat again."

The judge exploded. "You sentimental liberals give me such a pain in the ass. We're at war in this society and you milky kids think you can have it both ways. Grow up, Harry! You married my daughter! You've made it, boy!"

"You're so awful," Kate cried out. "I'm not you!"

She flinched as he looked at her, still not used to having herself replace her mother as the target of his profound contempt.

"I'll say you're not!"

In despair, Kate saw Elizabeth's father shuffle through the door, yapping briefly on the threshold like a well-trained dog. He banged against her, squeezed her hand, and tortured her bruised feelings with his wet, mournful eyes.

"Here's my favorite, my pretty, pretty niece. You look like a child in those jeans and shirt." He swung her hand and turned to the judge. "Do you remember, David, when she mowed the lawn in Maine for fifty cents? She barely topped the mower – it was an old wooden job – and the place hadn't been touched in weeks. She was so angry when I said she couldn't possibly cut the whole acre – damned insulted in her baseball cap and braids. I was so amused. She kept at it all day long and then wouldn't take a penny over what she had contracted for."

He stepped up to the judge and whispered loudly in his ear. "Who is this young fellow, David?"

Elizabeth had come up beside Harry, the hem of her tie-died gown spilling on his shoe as she offered hot cheese puffs on a silver tray.

Judge Edwards grouped the three young people negligently with a sweep of his hand.

"They're married, Chauncy, and I'm certain that come June they'll be delighted to cut your lawn."

With a suave smile, he took Elizabeth by the arm and led her off to talk with him before the fireplace. Harry made himself another drink and slipped around Mr. Graves and out the door. He sat on the dark stairs and gave Kate a sympathetic wave before settling gloomily over his drink.

Her uncle Chauncy was in a nostalgic mood. He pressed her hand and the sound of his mournful barking hurt her chest.

"Marriage is a sad thing," he said, "but you have a long, long ways to go before you have to think of that. Don't rush; enjoy your school days, that's the thing; they are the best part of life and they flow past, flow right past - leaving one high and dry and miserable."

"Why didn't Elizabeth's mother tell me she was getting married?" He barked indignantly. "He looked nice enough – huge fellow!"

Across the room, her head and shoulders hidden by the large, orange Chinese lamp, Mary Edwards shot out her thin arm, her empty glass pointing at her husband's broad back. She called his name but he was talking too intensely to Kate to hear her.

Striding out of the room, Chauncy barked a friendly welcome at Harry as he passed him on the stairs and Kate, finally free of him, mixed a whiskey and water, weak but not too weak, or her mother, drunk as she was, would send her back to the piano.

Mary Edwards poked her elbow into Kate's ribs.

"Your father is giving his sermon: 'Look to this day, it is the very life of life.'" She caught Elizabeth's eye and hoarsely whispered: "Hang on, darling."

Turning cozily to her daughter, she said: "Of course I agree that life is the very life of life, but what's so good about it?" She took Kate's hand. "Are you in love with life? I see by your tears that you're not."

Pressing her face against her mother's shoulder, Kate grieved. Her mother sat hunched in the corner of the couch, hunched in her thin skin and brittle limbs. Further back each passing minute, back in her handsome head, her gloomy cave, growling at her husband, who daily provisioned her with food and drink and, twice a year, dragged her out to stand her upright under the burning southern sun.

37

Repeatedly, Kate had asked her father why her mother was so bitter and so down. What had happened to her? Why? When?

Because, he always said, her ancestors were Lowland Scots. A melancholy heritage, nothing to worry about. "I mean, have you ever been to the Lowlands of Scotland? It's a miracle anyone survived, let alone laughed!" So, he told her, forget her mournful face and bleak ways. One might as well get upset about the weather.

Fierce, joyful barking filled the room. Mr. Graves caned his way to the fireplace, yapping, growling, frisking his shoulders. The judge steadied him.

"Well, David, the champagne will be up in a moment." He pushed free of the judge's patronizing arm and tottered against his daughter. "Ah, Elizabeth, get your young man. A toast to you both."

The judge looked incredulously at his wife and daughter. "The old bastard doesn't know the difference between a wedding and a wake."

"Don't hang back." The old man's voice quavered imperiously. "Young man, will you kindly step away from the door and take your bride by the hand?"

Elizabeth rolled her eyes and with a droll tilt of her head beckoned to Harry to take her hand.

The Irish maid offered champagne on a huge silver tray. Sighing with the weight, she stood before her trembling, grinning employer.

"Yip, yip, yip-yippee."

Slowly Elizabeth turned her grave eyes from her father's now-empty glass to the judge's bright, bubbling face.

"Happy days, children!" The old man drank from his

empty glass, then dully peered. "Well, damn! What's the meaning of this? Gave me an empty glass, she did. Fire her!"

The maid nudged her employer with the rim of the tray. "Have another go, Grandpa, you can call the agency tomorrow."

Mary Edwards laughed as Mr. Graves murmured grudgingly and took another glass. Kate had forgotten the sound of her mother really laughing. Robust, light, musical, it kept breaking from under her hand. The sound of it sent Harry racing from the room, his hand clapped over his mouth, and the judge into a quivering rage. He turned his back, drying his face and spectacles with his handkerchief.

Mr. Graves had begun to turn in circles, urgently barking over his left shoulder. Elizabeth took him by the hand and serenely walked him from the room.

"Wuff, wuff."

"Yes, a fine, good dog," came her calm, low voice. "You'll have a lovely biscuit and a bowl of warm milk before bed."

The judge gazed rancorously down at his delighted wife.

"Shut up," he growled.

Reluctantly, Mary Edwards got to her feet. "Ah, you've no humor. Listen to Harry. He's downstairs sounding like the rebel army."

"Harry doesn't have to sit at the crack of dawn."

She poked his out-thrust chest. "Dreadful David sits again."

The judge stalked off, tossing his head.

Mrs. Edwards put her arm around her daughter and leaned against the piano as Elizabeth wrapped a score of little sandwiches in napkins and put them in her big, shiny bag.

"Dear old Lizzy," she joked in an English movie voice. "You're so terribly queer. It would be quite the thing to go out to a restaurant on your wedding night, rather fun, I should think."

"I've had enough damned fun, Aunt." Elizabeth's voice and face were riotously sour. "God, fun is awful."

The judge stood in the doorway, wincing at the soft sound that escaped his wife.

"You farted, Aunt," Elizabeth glumly announced and did so herself.

"Inherit the wind, I always say." Mary Edwards roared at her own joke, then managed to cruelly knock her hip against the outreaching piano top as she moved towards the Judge.

Elizabeth helped her aunt down the stairs. When she came back through the door for her bag, she'd filled like a sponge with hard misery.

"Work," she croaked, shouldering her bag. "If you find another way out, Coz, be sure to tell me."

She rushed up the stairs to check once more with her father's nurse. Kate, crossing the hall, rehearsed her apology to the lean, dark woman for the drink she had not brought. She hesitated on the threshold, then took a brave step in. But the room was empty.

Picking *Pride and Prejudice* off the coffee table, Kate dropped down at the end of the couch, where the dark-booted lady had dented the soft cushion, and began to read.

The pages fluttered and the curtains covering the French doors shot out as Harry stepped into the room from the balcony. His heavy shoes slid on the polished step. His big head, his big shoulders drooped.

"God, you're really drunk," she said uncritically. His face brightened when he saw her. Very drunk, but graceful, nonetheless. At home he'd fold over chairs and for all his size and weight land lightly on the floor.

He sat on the arm of the couch. Leaning over her, he stared from exhausted eyes.

"I am a sentimental liberal."

"You're a fine, decent fellow."

Harry stroked her hair. "I love you."

"Likewise, but what are you going to do?"

"I'm going to make the biggest wave that I can and then swim like mad." He smoothed his hair. "How do you feel about being the wife of a football coach?"

"Let's go home." She took his hand. "I'll read to you in bed."

Harry squinted at the title. "I read something by Jane Austen once. I liked it."

Fast, light footsteps sounded on the stairs. Out of breath, pushing back her bangs, Elizabeth looked quickly around the room. She went out on the balcony.

"Margo?"

Elizabeth stepped back into the room. Her face was closed and defensive.

"Who's Margo?" Harry asked.

"A disloyal bitch!" Elizabeth stalked to the couch and took *Pride and Prejudice* from Harry's hands.

41

"I wasn't introduced." He turned to Kate. "Were you?"

"I met her," Kate said.

Elizabeth responded to her faintly boastful tone with a wink before heading out.

"Well, that makes us two of the luckiest chicks in town."

3

On the Upper East Side, walking toward the river, a young woman pushed a heavy baby carriage. Touching the brim of her cowboy hat, she smiled up at a friendly lady, who, leaning from a second-story window, had called down:

"Hi ya, cowboy!"

She walked broodingly behind the splendid blue carriage and at every corner examined through the handlebars her crisp, new leather boots and pre-faded Levi's. The young woman was Kate Stevens dressed up as Valery St. John.

She was afraid. A big, blue carriage sailed before her. In it, her baby. A girl called Cam, after the Cam in a book she loved, who was wild and fierce. Not afraid like herself. What was she so afraid of? Taking a new step? The young woman wished she knew. She did know that everything was in a woman's hands, that the time had arrived for her sex and therefore for herself and she earnestly wished she could do something other than watch the baby sleep and think of Wonderwoman.

This was the name she'd given to a lady painter, lean and dressed in black, whom she'd met a week ago at the funeral of her aunt. The memory of her gruff, mocking voice as it came through the telephone two nights before caused her chest to tighten with excitement.

"No, Elizabeth can not be called to the phone at

this moment or indeed at any moment for the next few days. She's off around the country on some law school business. "You can leave her a message, if you like."

Kate had then introduced herself.

"Kate Stevens? The famous cousin Kate? Well, I'll be sure to tack up your name on the message board and hope to soon have the pleasure of meeting you!"

Kate was meeting her today. The young woman squeezed the thick rubber grip of the carriage as her shoulders hiked up in a spasm of nerves. Valery St. John would adventure downtown that very afternoon.

Tramping behind the English carriage, her husband's western hat tipped back on her head, her shoulders drooped, she was on her way, in the wet, orange light of the early autumn morning to buy corned beef. Then she and Cam would walk on to the park.

In front of the meat market, children swarmed round the carriage and latched on. Each one wanted a tip for watching the shiny blue coach and, by the way, the tiny child, sleeping like a princess inside.

A pair of dirty hands appeared on the handlebar as a little girl, her hot head smelling sulfurous from the city air, hopped up on the brake and rode it down.

She was going to watch, she said, and glared under the handlebar at her jealous friends. Wild and fierce, Valery thought, looking back at the thin, gripping thing, but the little boys who now shied off would get her later, get her, most likely, for the rest of her life.

The pale green tiles of the butcher shop looked cool. The window of the meat case was sweating. Valery lolled against it, pulling the big furled brim of her hat down over her eyes. Dominic poured chicken livers into a carton, ignoring her. The heavy wooden door shot out and Dominic's father, the owner of the shop, stepped through, an animal's leg and thigh jutting on his shoulder. He winked at Valery

"How's the baby?" he asked, then roared at Dominic to get her a nice piece of corned beef on the double. He sawed through bone, his gory hands blue cold. "That Dominic is more trouble than a woman," he told her. "Doesn't like his soft musician's hands on the meat, doesn't want the long hours – he's ashamed to earn his living selling meat!"

A yell from outside. Valery walked to the window. Arms like pipes, the little girl shrieked at the others to stop rocking the carriage – they'd wake the baby! A harsh crowing as first a foot and then the top of Cam's blond head broke the edge of the carriage. Ha, ha! She'd awakened the baby! The girl's fit of hatred swept to joy as she saw Valery smile and wave. See, the lady isn't mad. She tossed her hot curls.

As Dominic held up the meat, Valery stared from narrow eyes, the counter glass running cold from her crotch to her armpits. Between the broad brim of her hat and the top of the counter she challenged his icy look.

"Will I have to soak the meat?" she asked, then felt, as he silently turned, the sullen wall of his head and shoulders.

His father spun round, whacking him on the arm. Valery felt her smile spread warmly on the glass. "Answer the lady!"

"Just tell me where the lady is," Dominic shouted, and I'll answer her. I don't see a lady in this shop..."

The old man pushed his son to the side, wrapped the corned beef in white paper, and tied it round and round with a red string. Presenting it to Valery with a gallant bow, he walked her out to the sidewalk to admire the baby.

"Beautiful, beautiful," he said, his thick fingers pressing his chest.

The little girl watched tensely as Valery dug in her pocket. Terribly tense she was, her huge eyes like glue on Valery's as she gripped the quarter.

Valery pushed off, heading east to the playground where she took her daughter, weather permitting, twice a day. But today it would just be the morning, for Mrs. Quinn was coming to care for Cam in the afternoon.

A mild wind was in her face, running off the river, smelling of rot and brine and yeast from the baker on the opposite shore. Huge trucks rattled wildly on the cobblestone avenue, filling the dull morning air with gas. When Harry smelled the air his green eyes would flash with panic. Was there such a thing as gas masks for babies, he'd once asked. They should check Abercrombie's, who knows but they might have a new line of survival gadgets for the deprived rich.

Ten o'clock on a Saturday morning as Kate Stevens entered the playground, disguised as Valery St. John. Ahead an iron fence sectioned the gray, grinding river, the city loomed behind. A slot on the bench near the sandbox and Valery went for it, her splendid buggy sweeping majestically across the bow of a frail cloth and iron pram. Valery glanced at its owner.

Hello, Cam darling! Another day, another dollar, and

the child was wet as a pig. Valery changed her and stuffed the urine-soaked diaper in a plastic bag.

Cam laughed with excitement and held up her arms.

This dull day, her eyes looked as dark as her navy blue sweater. Her daughter, whom she planted in one corner of the sandbox, whose strong hands grabbed the red plastic pail and shovel, whose broad head, as she passed her hand over, coated her palm with warmth.

As Valery sat down on the bench, paper crinkled in her back pocket. She drew out a letter, received this morning from the Feminists.

They thanked her for her interest, but they felt (the shaggy, snotty girls who'd interviewed her), they sincerely felt that the process of her radicalization had a ways to go before she could be an effective member of their organization. The problem, concretely, was her institutional alliance with a man. The Feminists had accepted married women in the past, only to find that their radicalism was too theoretical to be of much use to them.

Bitter, really bitter. Oh, yes, she'd had to ask about their current programs and who their leaders were – the put-down in those cold, young eyes had been too much – but emotionally, in her torn apart heart and mind, Valery St. John suffered the disgrace of femaleness.

Kate chewed her fingers. Had she been left out before she'd even begun? This morning she'd come out the front door with the garbage, picked the letter off the threshold, and gone on to the back hall. There, a mound of cold cornflakes fallen on her bare foot, she'd read that Kate Stevens, grown bleak in the gut, wasn't yet sufficiently liberated.

47

And those fuckers on the judgment seat were seven years younger, at least! She'd wept with rage!

Through the dark green service door she could hear Harry making breakfast in the kitchen. He'd need the garbage pail for the eggshells but she stayed and stared at the greasy mustard-colored walls, the stairwell rising dimly on her right. There, at the turn of the stairs, hung a fire ax. Her tears vibrated its red outline, the blade and handle irritating her eyes. Her hand crumbled the insulting letter and the thought occurred. What if she were to cut off her husband's head with that ax and bring it to those cocksure maenads in a plastic bag?

I have left off weaving at the loom for greater things – for hunting wild beasts with my bare hands. Do you praise me?

Her sullen, unblinking eyes freed the red of the ax handle from its outline, flowed it down the walls.

She climbed a few stairs, fitted her hand on the shaft, and pulled. The ax handle flew from the cleats, the blade diving, nearly slashing her leg. Back it fitted with a loud click, her stomach jumping at the sharp sound. Sweat dripping down her side, Kate carefully judged the best place for her hands.

If she were to conveniently lose the front door key, Harry would be obliged at the end of a long Saturday night to fiddle with the unfamiliar back door lock, to kneel perhaps with bowed head and then, the ax raised shoulder high, she'd steal behind him and release, as one would a stone, the head of the ax, letting it plunge of its own weight, letting it cut.

Cam howled, close behind the kitchen door. Kate whirled and stared at the dark green wood, feeling her eyes grow huge. Cam's loud wailing froze her to the spot. It was as though Harry's head hung in her bloody hand and she must stand there like a dumb cow to be caught and led away. Dumb cow, dumb cow!

Hurl that gory head into those young, contemptuous faces and march off to the slammer, one's problem of identity momentarily solved.

Back on the other side of the kitchen door, eating the breakfast that Harry had made for her, the wall that he'd painted rising brightly at her back, Kate fed Cam bits of pancake and regretted the little pantomime that had inexplicably plunged her beyond an ironical acceptance of her absurdity.

In the shoe store where she'd bought her boots, her sense of limitation and inadequacy, her isolation, were like choking hands on her neck.

A laconic female voice drilled in her dreaming ear.

"Is that your little girl? Is that your little girl?" In the sandbox, Cam was howling for her pail and shovel. Valery knelt on the concrete edge and looked a small, solid boy in the eye.

"Can you please give her back her pail?" Face, hand, and eyes gleamed stubbornness. Not yet two, Valery figured, and the kid shone with a king's will. One by one she unlatched his fingers from the pail, stuffed it between Cam's legs, and went back to the bench.

Christsake! Cam wailing, the boy tugging. Little bastard! Valery sprang.

"Cut it out!"

Stolidly, the boy pulled the pail from Cam's hands. Valery yanked hard. A faceful of sand for you, little fuck

– lace lord of the universe. Spitting sand, screaming, the little boy climbed backward out of the sandbox and ran to a woman with teased hair who lay sleeping on a broken park bench.

A delegation of mothers approached the broken bench. The waked mother sat up yawning. Look, look, cried the delegation, sand in his eyes, ears, nose, and throat. Valery stood negligently by the sandbox. The lady's nest of platinum hair glittered in the sudden sun. Sand in her baby's eyes!

Western-like, tipping back her hat, Valery said that she wasn't from this part of the country, no, sir! She sure wasn't used to defending her baby from kids twice her size, kids that wouldn't take no for an answer. Where she was from, the big ones were taught to look out for the squirts and had their little behinds skinned if they didn't. In hot pants and a halter top, the woman examined Valery from her boots to her hat, her eyes dipping back to her chest.

"Honey," she finally asked, "are you for real?"

"Sure am, ma'am."

The woman rolled her eyes, pushed out her cheek with her tongue, then went, hips smugly rolling, back to the bench and lay down.

Valery settled her hat, was aligning her boots, when she saw the little boy pick up the shovel and crack it flat down on Cam's head. In a flash the shovel was in her hand but clearly, in the heart of her fury, she saw a tiny judge and nine tiny jurors hating her, and didn't she land that shovel so carefully, just a pat upon the bully boy's head, a token tap.

"And that's how we teach 'em in Texas, honey!"

At the urging of the mothers, Blondie ran after the big, blue carriage, ran right out to the street, looking madly for a police car among the intercontinental trucks. Valery stood beside her, wondering if she should spit into that mass of tortured hair. A worthy gesture of Valery St. John?

"Ugly bitch," the woman yelled. "Ugly bitch with your stupid hat! You're crazy!"

Then a triumphant shriek: "Hey, you! Are you a man or a woman? Tell me that!"

Halfway across the broad avenue, Valery turned and cupped her mouth.

"I'm an idea," she yelled and strode on, grinning down at Cam.

If she did not spit into the consumer curls of a blond bitch who ranked her as a thing – those eyes had dipped twice to her ambiguous chest – if she, Valery St. John, hadn't kicked those hips in their insinuating swivel, it would more or less have to snow in hell before she managed the ax that knocked off Harry's head.

In the thundering, shrieking, wailing sorrow of the avenue – for you, Valery – we thunder, shriek, and wail for you – the tall, humiliated figure walked west.

Bullshit! Self-pity is the unpardonable indulgence. Why the hat, the boots, the faded Levi's? Why the navy blue jersey if not to sink through myth and meanness and find what you will find?

Crash! The gracious carriage shook violently, having abruptly contacted the awning post of the stately apartment house where Kate Stevens lived. Valery's stomach caved round the handlebar.

"A strap test, Cam, darling. Wasn't that fun? See why Mummy buckles you in? Ho, ho!"

Valery righted the baby, placed her hands on the side of the carriage, then hauling on the handlebar –

"Wait!" cried the elevator man – but she quickly drew the back wheels of the carriage up the three steps. Thick strands of saliva yo-yoed from Cam's happy mouth as Valery turned the large carriage and swept into the elevator.

In the elevator, Eddy playfully squeezed her biceps. Wasn't she the powerhouse! He pushed out the carriage, put a lemon candy in her back pocket for Cam, and said in his kind, clumsy way that he was glad to see that they hadn't taken her strength in the hospital.

The front door swung open before Valery turned the key. Tiny Mrs. Quinn beamed at Cam.

"Ah, there's my girl!" She pinched the child's cheek and, brushing Valery's sleeve, gaily teased: "Will you look at the getup on her?"

As Valery unharnessed Cam, she stood at the head of the carriage, her quick fingers drumming on the hood. Mrs. Quinn was Eddy's first cousin and for the past three months had come every afternoon to care for Cam.

"The shopping went quicker than I thought, so I just let myself in. Cam's lunch is ready and there's a chop for you, if you like." She smiled caustically. "That's a fine hat you've got on your head. Did you pick it out of the trash?"

Mrs. Quinn jogged Cam. "You need a wash, a change, and a good, big lunch." She walked briskly through the living room, Valery behind. High on Mrs. Quinn's shoulder, Cam grinned directly into her mother's face.

"See you," Valery whispered and ducked into her bedroom. She must go to the bathroom, then look up, while she still had the nerve, the address of Elizabeth's loft. Kate Stevens walked into the kitchen, took the pot from the stove, and waited at the sink while Mrs. Quinn rinsed Cam's dishes.

"What are you going to put in that big, iron pot?"

"I'm cooking corned beef for supper. It needs soaking."

Mrs. Quinn examined the meat. "This needs to start cooking around four. I'll put it in for you and leave the cabbage chopped. Eat your lunch now. I'll sit down with you and have my tea."

While Kate had found the address of Elizabeth's Chinatown loft in the phone book and written it down, while she'd brushed her teeth and scrubbed the niches of her anxious body, Mrs. Quinn had bathed and fed Cam and put her to play on the kitchen floor with a red enamel bowl and an eggbeater.

It was torture to eat, but Mrs. Quinn kept watching while she chewed and chewed the rubbery lamb. Cam crawled over to her mother's chair and hauled herself to her feet. The child's straight back and subtle, balancing hands were delightful. Following Kate's glance, Mrs. Quinn said that Cam was a beautiful child but that she was going to be big like her father.

"I like 'em big," said Kate, chewing.

"And where is Mr. Stevens today, that tall, handsome thing?"

"Working," Kate said, still chewing. Mrs. Quinn tapped Kate's wrist.

"Aren't you the lucky one to have such a fine, hard-

53

working fellow for a husband? And yet, he's so nice and handy around the house. And doesn't he love his daughter, forever feeding, changing, and playing with her?"

Mrs. Quinn stretched out her short, thin legs with a happy smile. "I get a real kick out of Mr. Stevens cooking the way he does, caring for the baby. My poor husband was the same kind, a big, tall fellow with a lovely smile."

Kate went to the fridge for a beer. Stepping over Cam, she sat down again and offered Mrs. Quinn a glass.

"Not for me, thanks, I'm happy with my tea."

Kate needed the beer, for she'd heard the story of John Quinn's long and ghastly death many times before. Life leaped high in Mrs. Quinn as she poured out the details. At the climax, her pale eyes wet with excited tears, she thrust her pink face so close that Kate could smell the sweet, warm tea on her breath.

"The last week, he was no bigger than a child and screaming when we had to turn him in the bed." She imitated the gruesome, hollow sound he'd made, her forefinger vibrating on her larynx.

"Low, it was, and far away. The cancer had gotten to his voice box, you see, eaten it right away. At the end it had eaten everything like a swarm of ants. The doctors couldn't believe there was life in him, thought it was a miracle. And the eyes on the man! He couldn't scream because there was nothing left to scream with, but his eyes were screaming, my God, you couldn't look into his eyes – "

She let go of Kate's hand, took a sip of tea. "His poor head kept stretching up, like this. Way, way back on the pillow with those screaming eyes as if he were trying to get

54

away." She shook herself, took more tea. "And wouldn't I be trying to get away? Oh, wouldn't I?"

As usual, Kate slammed her hand down on the table and smiled at Cam, who started at the sudden noise.

"Why didn't the bastard doctors stop the pain?"

As usual.

"Ah, Mrs. Stevens, at the end they were sticking the needles up through his feet." Had to be his feet, not a vein in his body that wasn't collapsed – vegetable hands and feet he had, for there was no oxygen getting through, his limbs just rotting on him, as if he were already dead."

Kate groaned. "They've got the drugs that can put you out. When things get rough they snow the patient. Shit!"

The old Irishwoman regarded her patiently. "But that shortens the life."

"What?" Kate shouted. "Shut up, Cam!" She picked up the wailing child. "Mrs. Quinn, what life are you talking about?"

Her thin fingers moved around the rim of the cup, then flew to her chest, drawing a cross.

"What if there was a miracle?"

"For a man on an anthill?"

Kate jogged Cam, got her quiet. She'd gone further this time, pulling Mrs. Quinn out of her depth and making her unsure. She watched the old fingers nervously circling the rim of the cup and said, as though to apologize.

"I had cancer."

Morbid excitement welled up in the old Irishwoman's eyes. She picked Cam off Kate's lap and covered the top of her broad head with mournful kisses.

"Ah, Mrs. Stevens, I didn't know."

"It was cancer of the breast," Kate stoutly said.

"Did they operate?"

Kate looked sharply at the old woman. Hadn't she really noticed?

"They took the left breast."

"It could have been worse, love." She stood up with Cam. "Thank God they caught it. Eh?" She put Cam down beside the red bowl, rattled the eggbeater on the rim, then cleared the table. "Thank God, they caught it."

She washed the plates, her heavy breasts shaking beneath her cotton dress, then turned to the baby.

"And now, what will our little girl have for her supper?"

Kate, finishing her beer, kept her eyes on the light, vigorous gestures, for although they'd taken off the entire left breast, there remained, a slight, vicious chance that the cancer might recur. But that would take five years. The young woman left the kitchen and stared at herself in the full-length mirror attached to her bedroom door. And five years was longer than a lifetime.

Valery adjusted the brim of the cowboy hat and turned sideways. Her navy blue turtleneck jersey, gray tweed jacket, and leather shoulder bag were all good, but the hat was dumb. She took it off and flung it on the broad bed behind her.

"Good-bye, Mrs. Quinn. Bye, Cam. Anon!"

4

Down the avenue an adolescent boy dragged her in his bounding stride. Listening to his heels on the smooth pavement, she matched her step to his. Like him, Valery St. John was tall, thin. Broad-shouldered, narrow in the hip, she had a strong, athletic body that she could thank her mother for.

At fifty-three her mother had lost her strength, but last week, passed out cold on the living room rug, her body, released from conscious tensions, had spread out majestically on the ancient Persian scene. Wheeling away, the daughter acknowledged her debt and vowed. Vowed what? The tall, fast, striding female wished she knew.

Sunlight. Canyoning the narrow avenue, the glossy buildings shot her exercising eye into the dazzling blue air. Far above the dark, congested gorge – it stank on this river's edge and one's ears rang with vicious sound – was a corridor of silent blue and sailing there a wedge of seagulls. Above them, its velvet voice preceding, a jet cruised down.

A fairy image of high, brick, ivy-covered walls and rooftop gardens veiled the top of her eye as she plunged down subway stairs, down, down below ground. At the change booth, the grating rattling in the roar of the incoming train, Valery held up two fingers and shouted at the woman in the token booth.

"Two, please!" Two gold coins spun over wood into her hand.

Thank you. Valery glanced. A bird in a cage; a woman saying, "Welcome," caged in the dark.

The gold coins clicked. Her sharp hips spun the wooden gate. Welcome! The track filled with train, the doors parted, the girl departed.

Although there were seats, the young woman with her serious, fine-boned face did not sit but stood within reaching distance of the center pole. This morning Harry had told her that Elizabeth had been sent to the Midwest to recruit law students. And yet, the young woman, all dressed up, was tripping to Chinatown to see her cousin.

A fast curve. She bent, leaned, her feet maneuvered slightly as she read – the headline blaring up at her – *JAMES EATON KILLED IN GUNFIGHT*. She was shocked. A young African American leader, one of the best. Harry had made her read his book. He'd written it in prison and now he was dead.

To Valery, the thick-walled prison cities were monasteries where stately black men wrote their autobiographies. Once she had demonstrated at the women's prison. She remembered how, responding to the shouting demonstrators on the sidewalk below, a flock of dark arms had shot out from barred windows, the arms of hundreds of women, flapping – but the building didn't budge.

At the City Hall station the young woman got out. In the dim, low, subway tunnel, huge posters flashed by. Up a short flight of stairs and on the wall a bright, heterosexual love scene. The young woman stopped before it, brooding.

In the foreground of a medieval scene of castles and visored, clashing warriors, two heads were fused at the lips of the female bent, the male bending.

The young woman walked on. At the head of the stairs, the light of the street just beyond, loomed a poster sky where helmeted American warriors rode their choppers. Two heads floated in the blue, the male bent, the female bending.

Again, Valery stared. Twenty years ago, even fifteen, not much touched by herself or others, hadn't she thrilled to a scene like this? Bona fide in sneakers and Levi's, hadn't she thrilled and thrilled and thrilled to the female bent, the male bending?

Pathetic! She was over twenty before she realized that the vivid buzzing of her desire was unconnected with that final surrender, the forced-apart lips, the arching neck. Hideously disappointing, the wet pressure of male lips on hers. In her case, the kiss of the prince had put her to sleep and she was sleeping still.

The young woman opened her leather bag and took out a pen. Quickly, skillfully, she drew tears in the huge female eyes and ran them down her cheeks.

Kate Stevens had grown to hate her imagination, which sustained itself claustrophobically outside of experience. She knew nothing of enlightened girls and boys or even of communities outside her own. All she knew was that her father had pushed her into the closet of Wall Street law and had tried to lock the door. Well, fuck him! She was out, dressed, and on her way. She stopped just short of the Oriental arch, the curve of Chinatown beyond.

Would it be all right? Could it be all right to come downtown costumed in her finest conception?

Valery dug in her pocket for the address. Carefully she walked along among the newly-planted Asian community toward the elevated train a block away.

Elizabeth's loft was on this avenue, near the elevated train. She and Harry had come to Elizabeth's housewarming a year before but she had not paid attention. They'd eaten dinner with Elizabeth and a few of her friends, surrounded by cartons in a huge, gloomy space. Just out of the hospital, depressed, and on guard, Kate had not felt the least curiosity about why Elizabeth should give up her two pleasant rooms near the university for a walk-up with grimy, desolate ceilings and windows that bore bars.

Now she walked past dim, glass windows that showed bags of grains and things like harnesses, hanging from walls. A strong smell of apples in the wind and Elizabeth's doorway, as she stepped inside, smelled of fresh wood shavings. Nineteenth-century sights and smells and then, a block beyond, the passing of an elevated train shook the panes of glass in the heavy steel door. She stepped outside and read the lettering "American Radiator Company." Yes! Elizabeth was settled on the top floor.

The stairs climbed for two long flights at a time, went round a landing, and stretched on again. Up and up. Broad, shallow steps that led through smells of wood shavings, paint, and turpentine. Valery began, her boots softly scrubbing the wood. Her chest boomed as she climbed and deep in her stomach something cold and bright began to feel.

At the top of the building, in the dim, paint-smelling hall, Valery rapped aggressively on the steel door, rapped again, then, terrified by the persistent silence, collapsed on the top step, forced her lungs into her freezing gut, and began to breathe.

Dignity streaming from her legs, she descended. An old wreck hobbling down, chucked out into the boring day. Hands in her pockets, she shoved off from the step, shuffled east.

A tall figure swayed in front of her, blocking her path.

"And what might you be doing in this part of town?"

A tall, dark figure swayed in her path with the wind blowing cold behind her. A dusky pea jacket with the high collar drawn up, the broad brim of a black Spanish hat drawn down, and glasses looming at her, murky as pitch.

Valery stepped back, jiggled, would have run, but a large hand flashed from a pocket and caught hers.

"Kate Stevens, how sweet." The dark lady pulled her around, tugged her back toward the steel door. "You've come calling on Elizabeth, but, alas," (a backward grin, a startling gap in the toothy grin) "our mutual friend isn't at home."

Upward bound in the dim shaft, the dark lady hauled them both along, her pewter ring clicking on the banister as she gripped. She'd just been out to lunch and lost her false tooth on the steak sandwich; fell right onto the floor and rolled through the grill of the radiator.

She dug in her pocket for keys and quickly opened the door. "By Christ, if those fuckers have shut me down – "

She strode to a panel of switches. Wang! The huge, white space bloomed with light. Valery pressed back against the door and shaded her eyes. The imposing figure unbuttoned her coat, sailed her hat onto a yellow couch, and gave a quick, proud glance at Valery as it neatly landed.

"You look cold," she said. "Come in the kitchen and I'll give you some brandy."

She pulled Valery to a small space at the end of the loft, drew a chair from the round kitchen table, and bade her sit.

"No brandy? Well, I'm going to have some. Tea, then? Good!" She put on the kettle, politely excused herself, then passed an age in the bathroom.

Valery set cups out on the wooden table, found tea bags, poured in the boiling water, then poured it out as it grew stone cold. Boredom flattened her nerves and she explored the loft, drastically changed since her visit a month ago. In the place of Elizabeth's garden sofa and chairs, now pushed way back from the huge loft windows, was a cluster of work lights, tables covered with jars and brushes, and dozens of canvases piled against one another along the wall.

The young woman prowled, then froze, her hands flying to her eyes in the violent assault of light. From the darkness beyond, a deep, authoritative voice commanded her: "Step up on that platform, please, and turn toward me."

Valery stepped up, turned, then fretted. She should never have let herself become the blind, dumb target of the painter's unseen scrutiny. The artist stepped up to the platform. Gallantly, in a lilac shirt, she guided Valery down the steps, her collar, as her arm came up, opening to her waist. On Valery's quickly averted eye, a refined, brown breast had burned its image. Half choking, she asked the painter's name.

"Margo Schwartz," she replied. "Now, please turn yourself around and tell me what you think of this."

As the young woman obeyed, the painter's hands clinked on her shoulders and a light, spicy perfume filled her nose.

An enormous canvas faced her, the wooden frame and thick braces reflected in a giant mirror fastened to the wall behind. Up and up she looked, her mind sputtering, her senses filled to the brim with the imposing glory of big.

"So big," she finally said. The ringed hands pressed her shoulders.

"Come on, come on!" The painter wanted more of her first impression.

Big eyes, nose, mouth, chin. The painted buttons on the man's shirt were the size of nickels; the wrinkles and folds on the jeans were mountains and valleys in groovy configurations. Valery ducked the hands and walked back. The painter turned, watching her look. Weird. Behind the flesh-and-blood Margo a giant Margo loomed, both dressed in shirt and jeans. As the living Margo waited for an answer, her face took on the expression that was so hugely rendered in the painting. The tough, cocky, ironic expression came at her double and Valery began to laugh.

"It's terrific," she said. "I love it!"

Margo's penciled brows cocked suspiciously. "You do?"

"Oh, yes!" As Valery compared the real and the

63

painted face, she began to see, in the set of the jaw and the tense mouth, another look, like another face, swimming up through the shallows of jaunty aggression; an exhausted, beaten, disgusted face lay behind all the pluck and courage, lay waiting.

"I'm in love with it," she quietly said.

"Well, don't look so sad," Margo cried. "It's going to be seen at our great museum's annual show of contemporary American artists. Who knows but this aging tomboy may be on her way, if the fucking light company leaves me alone."

Valery sat at the kitchen table and drank tea. Margo drank brandy with her feet up.

"I don't blame the kids for blowing up the town; goddamn bureaucracies, they're killing us. Just five minutes after Elizabeth toted her chic little traveling case out of here, the fuckers are on the phone and telling me that they've got nothing better to do today than swing on downtown and turn off my lights."

The lilac band of her man's shirt looped out with her gestures and flattened back. Valery blocked the occurrence with a polite hand. Distracted, sweating, she inquired after the motives of the lighting company. Margo smiled sociably.

"Why, they haven't been paid in six months, poor babies! I told them I'd be delighted to run uptown with a check this very morning except for a wee problem. I explained that I have a joint checking account with my roommate, who had most inconsiderately taken the checkbook out of town – on her delightful person, as it were. And when, they asked, would my husband be back?

64

I politely explained that I wasn't married, was appalled, in fact, by the very idea of marriage, and that my partner for now and for checks was a perfectly lovely lady by the name of Elizabeth Graves."

Margo poured herself another brandy and knocked it back.

"Didn't we have two checkbooks, they asked? Of course we do, quoth I, but one is lost, mine, and the other is at present on the person of my good friend Graves. I am a painter, I tell them, getting ready for a show. I need every bit of light I can get, so please, I plead, would they be so kind as to wait a day or two until the lady of the checkbook reappeared? They would not. They would be down before nightfall, the fucking lords of darkness." Margo glared at the fridge.

"There's half a cow in the freezer. Elizabeth will die."

Valery reached under the table for her bag. "Would they take my check?"

"Hell, honey, they want a hundred and fifty bucks."

"I can cover that." Valery laid her checkbook on the table.

Margo clapped her hands. "Really?" Her legs dropped off the table with a bang. "Make it out to Margo Schwartz." She came around the table and stood watching over Valery's shoulder. "Oh, divine!" She slipped the check off the table and kissed it. "I'll rush right out to my favorite Chinese hardware store and be saved." She lunged over Valery and solidly kissed the top of her head.

They strode through Chinatown, arm in arm. Margo gaily bullied Mr. Wong, the friendly hardware man, to cash the check, then stepped onto the crowded pavement, her back pocket stuffed with bills.

"Let me walk you to the subway station."

They walked under the Oriental arch and past the housing development. At the top of the subway steps, Margo kissed her cheek.

"Kate, would you consider posing for me?"

The young woman considered a moment. "Yes, I would." She returned a warm smile from the artist.

"They asked if I could show two paintings and now, thanks to you, I think I can." She said excitedly. "Can you begin Monday?"

"Yes!"

"And you won't duck out once I've begun?"

"Never!"

Plunging down the subway stairs, Valery St John turned and looked up. The tall, dark lady stood against the movie poster, calling. Her shoulders and broad-brimmed hat blocked off the American warriors and Valery's view of the two heads fused at the lips, the female bent, the male bending.

"What?" Valery shouted up.

"Do you know the way home?"

5

The smell of corned beef filled the apartment. Harry had drawn the living room curtains and turned on the lights. He'd put wineglasses on the table and the silver candlesticks.

Valery walked through to the hall, smelling the cold, autumn night in the tweed of her gray jacket. Three doorways opened round her, showing bright walls beyond – blue, yellow, red.

Against Cam's red wall Valery saw a section of crib. Above, the king and queen of the elephants waved their handkerchiefs to the newborn child. Gaily stenciled letters said: "Hi, Cam!" This was Elizabeth's present to her godchild – a scene copied from the story of Babar.

From the blue square came Harry's soft, southern voice. Flat against the wall, straining her eyes to the right, Valery could see the end of the king-sized bed, and the side of the early American desk, its patina gleaming from Harry's drunken polishings.

"Ax, ax, cut, cut," Harry read. Cam yelped with pleasure. The desk was a wedding present from Kate's parents and Harry toiled grimly before it, not a willing scholar but a teacher forced by a status-crazy administration to publish. His stern, dark books and yellow pads spread out from the desk like islands on the soft green rug.

Valery peeked past the door frame. Stretched out on

the broad bed, a martini on the table beside him, and the spirals of cigar smoke fixing Cam's gaze, Harry read fairy tales in his T-shirt and shorts. He'd taken a shower and his shampooed hair sprang up in tight curls, the ends like a mass of tiny snakes dancing round his head.

He stopped reading, drank, sighed.

"A good man got murdered today. You know that, Cam honey? His people are damned mad and I don't blame them. Willy Hay – he's the main man in the African American Students' group – came in to see my boss. He wants the school shut down for a day, in honor of the man who was murdered."

Harry finished his drink and blew three perfect smoke rings. Cam crawled up his chest, stretching nobly with a wet mouth.

"You know what, Cam darling? Our distinguished dean wouldn't even see him. Can you believe it? I had to face Willy Hay myself and tell him how our Dean didn't consider him important enough to include in his schedule."

Harry blew a smoke ring right into Cam's hand. "I'm here to tell you, honey, that I was looking trouble right in the face. Jesus Christ! I never saw a man so mad in all my life and I don't blame him."

He sniffed and made a face. "Lord, lady, you were brand new just a minute ago. Come on. You get a wash, a bottle, and then it's bed."

Valery dashed back through the apartment and softly opened the front door. When Harry and Cam came into the kitchen she reentered, the door banging loudly behind her.

Kate struck a pose in the kitchen door, gave Cam a

Roman salute, then swept her off the floor and hid behind her warm, solid body.

Slipping by with the bottle, Harry gave her a pat on the ass. "You look good, kid."

Kate went behind him, carrying Cam. She took the dirty diaper as Harry peeled it off and washed it out in the toilet. Playfully parting Cam's strong legs, Harry cleaned her with cotton, then wrapped round a clean diaper. Lying on her back, her foot banging against the slats, Cam sucked her bottle. So triumphantly angled-Roland blowing in the pass, oh, king and country!

Kate stroked Cam's warm, bright head. Good night, sweet child. Good night, good night! Harry set a martini on the wide rim of the sink, smiled pleasantly, and stretched out on the bed.

Two swallows of gin and she felt so high. Cheerfully she lied about meeting Margo Schwartz outside the lighting company on Lexington Avenue.

"Who's that now, honey?" asked Harry.

"You remember me telling you about that sinister, booted lady who read Jane Austen all through the funeral? The woman who'd turned out to be Elizabeth's roommate – the painter?"

"She's desperately getting ready for a show and was about to have her lights turned off – " Kate clipped back her hair and stepped into the tub. "So, I gave her a check for the amount."

Harry put down the john seat and sat. "What amount?"

Kate sank in the hot water. "A hundred and fifty bucks."

"Good Christ!"

"Oh, hell," Kate smiled casually. "The lady is living with Fort Knox." She drowned her breast. "She wants me to pose for her. She likes my face."

"So do I."

"I don't," she snapped, then quickly said: "It's awful about James Eaton."

While Harry told her how Willy Hay had been humiliated by the dean, Kate cowered beneath the water and finished her drink.

"I asked Willy to lunch in an effort to ease a bad situation, but it's like he turned another side to me," said Harry, with a note of anguish. "He was cold and impersonal, as though *I* was a political enemy!"

Under the water, Kate's stomach was hot with gin. Blood banged through the thick artery under her hand while Margo's handsome shoulders and opening lilac shirt swam through her mind. Her nipple and stomach tingling, in a rage she lashed up through the water and stepped out of the tub. She bore an instant of Harry's gaze before flying the towel around her neck.

In the bedroom Kate stood, yanking the snarls from her thick hair. Her full image loomed in the mirror.

Behind it, Harry's large body was again spread over the bed, his watchful eyes like bright leaves in the glass. Her vigorous arm inched the towel from her shoulders and down her back. Soon Harry would see the thick scar shrieking under her armpit, would see the violent mode by which her trick chest had been created. The playful, androgynous effect so appreciated by Kate's myth-loving mind was lost. Mortality leered, the scar flashing like a serpent into the consciousness.

70

Harry brought her another martini and she sipped it sullenly.

"I read that liquor's rotten for the skin."

Harry laughed. "Your hairdresser told you that smoking pot caused split ends."

"She also said it would make me frigid." Kate ripped but a snarl. "Make me frigid, that's a laugh. I was born frigid."

She saw Harry wince as she tore at her hair. Kind green eyes, gaily arching brows, and blond, curling hair.

What was he doing, down in the reeds by the river?

His well-cut ears lay flat against his curls and didn't fill with reedy notes but Bach and rock – on weekend nights he cleared his head with strong vibrations and put down sexual panic with gin. It wasn't easy fucking the snow queen and the memory of the awful cold made it harder, week by week. Drunkenly she'd barge around the bedroom, railing and wailing. Why wouldn't this freeze let up? Feel, feel, she wanted to feel!

Always, Harry stuck by, watching her with troubled eyes. She must be kinder to herself, he'd say. Why did she insist that she was worse than the rest of humanity? If she could just learn to see herself the way he saw her – God, how could she bear her own brutality?

I have left off weaving at the loom for greater things – for hunting wild beasts with my bare hands. Do you praise me?

It was Friday night, so Kate pulled her black velvet hostess gown off the hanger, her hands attacking the armholes.

Kill her oppressor? Such shit! Would an Arctic people spite the sun? Some nights Kate would wake up and wonder when Harry would finally leave her to die under her blankets of snow. Breathing as he breathed, she coasted the long night against his calm back.

"You've eaten one string of meat and a cabbage leaf!" Harry noted. Kate smiled at him through the candlesticks and drank up her wine.

"God damn it, honey, you don't eat enough to keep a bird alive!"

She pushed her plate away, refilled her glass. "I adore this wine, it goes so well with cigarettes."

"This is the stuff your father gave us. It costs as much as Scotch."

Kate toasted him. "It's terrific. So are you terrific! Listen Harry, so what if this political thing risks dragging you down, you'll have stood by your ideas – "

"Glub, glub, glub?" He looked at her piteously. "Help! What is so stale as the breath of an unfed lawyer?"

"An uneasy conscience, babe! Just think, Harry, you've been working for something you believe in!"

The two candles burned a tent from the high darkness of the room. The blue smoke of Harry's cigar spiraled around their glowing skin and disappeared in the black beyond. All evening, in her elegant gown and neat gold slippers, Kate Stevens emptied her glass and ruggedly listened to her husband's torment. Whenever the noble shoulders of Margo Schwartz ducked out of the way, her attention was keen and sympathetic.

The thought that it was possible to succeed Dean Bender at the end of the year as the youngest dean in the history of the law school was suddenly put into a new light.

"You know, they may be using the deanship to box you up. Your job will be to settle fights, but there won't even be any, since the principal fighter – you – will now be the referee. In his brooding mood, her brightness struck him as offensive.

"There would be fighters," he challenged.

"Oh, yes? And there are plenty who won't see you as dean unless the new program students are gone, or at least the ones who would fight." He glowered at her.

"What makes you think that if I become dean I couldn't do whatever I damn well wanted to?"

"With all the senior faculty against you? You'd be out within the year!"

He lowered his head, the golden boy, who'd been picked so often and risen so fast. This startling momentum was the only narcotic his intense ambition had found. The rise could be purely formal, the contents behind the honor quite insipid, but, just as with Kate's father, it was the rise that momentarily calmed.

Harry slammed his hand down on the table. Dreaming of Margo's dynamic breasts, Kate glared at him. How dare he pound the table that way!

"What's the matter with you?

"Damned old men," he fumed. "Clear them all out!" He took up the casserole dish; she followed with the plates and put them in the sink.

"I suppose if Willy and his student band do something illegal, like take over a building, it would let you off the hook"

He crowed, his arm thudding around her shoulders. "You ain't the good judge's daughter for nothing."

She punched him. "Careful. You should have seen the expression on your face when my father told you, you could be dean – a fanatic excitement!"

He carried in the candlesticks, his green eyes mocking her above the leaping flames.

"Big reformer," she snarled. "What about that dream you had the other night?"

He belched. "What dream, honey?"

She blew an imaginary trumpet.

"The one when you were crowned king of the world?"

"In a cathedral yet."

She took hold of his shirtfront. "Trumpets, you fool. Choirs and long, long processions." He laughed delightedly.

"Cam was an angel flying around my head."

"Carrying a jewel-studded crown." She jabbed at him. "Don't forget the crown." He danced out of her reach.

"You're just mad because you weren't in it."

She went after him. "Because I'm the censor, right?"

Harry could drink all night and still she could never get by his guard.

"That's just the normal outpouring of a healthy ego."

"It takes confidence to have a dream like that." Her arm slashed through empty air. "I'd never have that dream because, you bastard, I have no confidence!"

Harry stumbled against Cam's high chair. His left dipped and her fist dove into his stomach. He eyed her coldly.

"You're dancing around like the gal who came in here dressed in boots and pants."

"You didn't like the way I looked, did you?" She pulled herself up on the counter.

He carefully rolled up his sleeves. "I suppose I don't much like you acting like a tomboy when you're dressed the way you are now."

"Oh, shit!" she sneered.

Suddenly Harry was standing very formally at the sink. Kate watched him pour the soap, lower the dishes. She listened to him breathe and felt the kitchen walls grow thick. Her stomach ached at the sight of his big Rose Bowl hands moving so carefully on the dishes.

Nothing she could say to him now would bait him into a fight. He was now the southern gentleman of his half admitted dreams and nothing would deter him from the evening's goal.

Kate drew her leg up and looked at her blister. Touching it, Margo's gay, tough face mocked her.

"Elizabeth's a fraud, you know."

Harry looked at her mildly. He held his hands under the faucet, where they turned and turned. "I didn't run into Margo Schwartz," she shouted. "I went downtown to see her."

As Harry placed the dishes in the rack, his gestures looked disgustingly soft, his full mouth disgustingly ripe as he murmured: "She must have made a big impression on you."

Kate pushed past him and took up the garbage pail. She faced him, clutching it to her stomach. "I stayed all afternoon and I'm going back Monday to pose for her."

Harry drew a chair from the kitchen table, sat down, and crossed his legs. So mild, so slow!

"Why did you say that Elizabeth was a fraud?"

"Because she is."

"Well, why?" he cheerfully asked.

Kate put the garbage down, grabbed it up.

"Elizabeth's turned her place into a studio and you don't go to those lengths for a normal roommate."

Sweet reason lit his open face. "You do if your roommate's a painter."

"Oh, shit, Harry, you're dumb!" Kate stormed the kitchen door, slammed it closed behind her. The garbage jammed in the throat of the incinerator. Furiously, Kate punched it clear. Big, dumb, soft man!

Kate flew to the ax. A pretty bow she made it. *Ah, my darling, would you care to dance?*

Pressing the heavy metal head to her cheek, Kate struck out. As she waltzed on slow, numb legs, Harry came into the hall and knelt before the green kitchen door. Soft, soft, breathing as he fitted in the key. What was he doing, doing, doing? On his knees, his curls pressed flat against the grim, green door, what was he doing in her fantasy?

"What is he doing?" she whispered to the ax. "You jammed the lock, cunt. The door won't open from the kitchen."

Behind him, Kate held the ax at arm's length and stood, feet stalwart, shoulders proud, the noblest sentinel.

Harry was still on his knees in an attitude of something. Curly curls curling. My! A fornication of serpents, yikes! Quite obscene really, quite uncalled for.

"Ax, ax, cut, cut," said the soft southern voice and the little girl yelped with delight to see the censor's ax come down. Arms, legs, trunk, cunt, hardening. Hard as the bright, red shaft Kate held in her hands. When asked why she'd done it, the unrepentant murderess would smile serenely and say nothing.

Kate bent, the ax fell across her foot; she groaned.

Behold the censor! Labia major et minor – to go among that mess of snakes – a woman ran forward and none could stop her, so strong was her sorrow. She held up the handsome head, the piteous, pale head of the savior, for all to see.

Kate stood the ax on its head and leaned. One hand on her hip, its pewter armada flashing under fierce lights, Margo sauntered up and looked down indifferently at the slit, gold slipper.

"What an asshole you are, twice an asshole, I should say. Bad enough to spill your own blood, but drown in it? Look at all that lovely, high-powered stuff surging through your slipper. Do something, will you?"

"Open!" Kate yelled, and hobbled into the kitchen, hoisting her leg to the table, and sitting down with a crash.

"Is that you?" asked her husband from behind the open fridge door. "Damn tray's frozen solid."

Kate folded back the long, heavy velvet skirt. Blood dripped through the slit in her golden slipper, pooled on the table, then hit the floor leisurely, poing, poing, poing.

Harry hammered, Harry swore, then appeared, a nostalgic blur to her death-sighted eyes. Kate grabbed at his hand, feeling no warmth in the contact.

"Jesus Christ," she croaked. He took his hand away. "Where are you going?" she cried. "Can't you see I'm almost dead?"

He ran the water behind her. "My hand's stuck to the tray – yah!"

Kate regretfully stared at the still-dripping blood, then Harry's big head blocked the gory view.

"You've cut your toe," he remarked.

"Off!" she snarled.

He glanced back at her. No off-ness in his gay, green eyes. He filled a bowl with warm water and said he'd scout for a Band-Aid.

She gasped: "A Band-Aid?"

"I don't know how you did it, but the skin's sliced off." He held open the slit in the slipper. "See? It isn't deep. Of course, I know it hurts."

Alone, suddenly bored, Kate brooded, felt the ceiling on her head and the walls against her back and chest, felt herself framed; a portrait. Young woman with matronly styled gown transfixed by bloody toe. Eyes wide, lips drawn down in line of sad speculation. Viewer impatient with the indwelling face, the harsh, self-hating eyes. Why so humorless, so seriously obsessed with security, identity, and the meaning of things? Dumb fuck!

Harry washed her leg and toe. He dabbed the Band-Aid with first-aid cream and wrapped it neatly around. As she hobbled from the kitchen, Kate heard him putting ice in glasses and the glasses on a tray. His big, careful hands would turn off the lights, turn her off, too. But that wasn't fair. She knew that wasn't fair.

She softly sang:

"Oh, he comes bearing Scotch and the darkness swims behind him. Oh, he comes in the dark with the bottles clinking round him."

Kate stopped at Cam's door. Was it a Friday or a Saturday fuck, she wondered, that resulted human?

Such a dear human. But not another. Oh, no! Modern technology played Thermopylae to her ingress.

The young woman stepped out of her velvet gown and limped to the bathroom, where she pressed her loins against the cold, white sink. She leaned there, glooming. Dumb fuck!

Behind the flecks of soap and shaving cream, just above the reflection of multicolored toothbrushes spraying from a red plastic cup, Kate worked an image from the dirty mirror. Dark skin stretched on fine warrior bones. A woman's face, possessed with the saga of the sword; stubborn, challenging eyes.

"Outrun, outshoot, outfuck! Yes, I can! Yes, I can. " Smash! Get the broad out of here. Swish, thump! Back through the swinging doors. Hi ho! A gun, then, a bomb!

Kate talked to herself, her breath filming up the mirror. "Margo Schwartz has nerve! Got real guts in that lean body. I have fantasies. I have the loathsome albatross, all day, all night."

Kate wiped off the mirror, gravely cocked her head, and was now brightly talking on a talk show, talking all night long. *But you see, it's really so clear, that in every male child there is a hero who will slowly emerge, while in every girl there sprawls a hero who is not invited, who punched the slighter lover out and took her place. This is the problem.*

Kate breathed deeply and stared into her own eyes. Harry would come back and find her drowning behind the bathroom door. She pressed her forehead, her cheek, then her lips against the glass.

"Who are you?" she whispered. "Who?"

The rug Agamemnon trod upon was red. Kate's was

soft green. Stepping into his tub, he changed the water into wine.

Kate stepped up to the bed. "Hi ya, pal." She hurled the blankets to the floor. Sailing the sheet, she jumped under and stretched out. It settled like snow on her fallen body, on her head.

Harry's light and modest step was in the hall. The clink of a glass on the table beside her, a pat for her hooded head. Kate winced, then held her breath to the count of four. How, now? A whiff of fish from her freshly washed notch?

It grew dark under the sheet as Harry clicked off the ceiling lamp, then faintly light again as the light of the bathroom poured through the half-open door. Kate fitted a pillow to the back of her head, looked out at her husband, carefully fitting the cuffs of his trousers over the edge of the top bureau drawer. The freshly washed ball of his hair narrowed his neck, making it thin and boyish in proportion. He stayed so long at the bureau.

One night, when he'd dropped onto her, she'd glimpsed his panicked eyes – she should have stopped him, but she dared not live colder than before. Now he lay outside the sheet in his T-shirt and oxford blue cotton undershorts. He pulled the pillow from under her head. His fingers, to compensate, lightly stroked her forehead. He'd thrown the blood-soaked sponge in the garbage, he said. Why had she taken the ax off the wall?

Kate sighed. "It occurred to me that the act of cutting off your head might win me a place in the movement."

He hoisted himself, his fingers falling from her forehead. "Kill me, your friend and lover, your faithful old nurse?"

She grinned, took some gin.

His fingers curled around her neck. "Get your murderous little body over here."

The first touch of his lips and chest and legs made Kate hot. She hooked onto him, sucking his tongue, pressing her stomach against his penis.

Always a brief period of fierce pressure between them as Kate struggled to feel Harry inside her by her own movements. He was so heavy, lying on her like fate, panting that he loved her. Sometimes she'd push against him and whisper that he should let her move, but running as he was to accomplish the deed in the snow, he was too possessed to hear and she too bleak to persist.

Bobbed right up after a fast orgasm, he did. Up and on his feet at the count of five. His head weighted her chest as, on his side, he threw his heavy leg across her and flamed up her clitoris with light and skillful fingers. For a minute the resistance of her mind acted as a stimulant. Kate became a tough, weathered woman drawn tight round the wet, frightened back of Harry stallion. The whip, the spurs, wheeled him up, bore him cruelly down. Tough old bitch! Not a horse in the country could throw her.

They'd both have another drink and he'd move down her body in a rush. The tip of his tongue on the ridge of her clitoris was a faithful pilgrim, uphill and down, uphill and down, until Harry's assumed impatience would embarrass Kate and make the contact so irritating she'd pull roughly away. Red in the face, tears in her eyes, she'd explain to Harry that she could not exact coolie labor for what was, after all, just an orgasm.

"Don't you understand that I love to do it?

"Hour after hour? Good Christ, no, I don't" Hurt and frustrated, he'd move off her, pull on his shorts, and smoke cigarettes, a yard of white away.

Kate balanced her glass on her flat bosom, spun the ice cubes round. "You should divorce me, you know." The glass rode her chest with such false complacency. Would he really trek south, leaving her to die, like the dinosaurs, under mountains of ice?

"Stop talking shit."

"The first time we went to bed together was a romantic's nightmare" – she slightly smiled – "but you thought it would get better."

He grabbed her hand. "I love you, nut! Things have gotten better. Better and better."

"Not in the sex department."

"Football players in my part of the country get a lot of tail. I've fucked around a lot with gals who moaned and groaned and acted like they were coming before they even got their clothes off."

She sat up. "You never told me that."

"Of course I've told you that! You have no memory! That's been your bedtime story for the past two years."

"Tell me again. I love to hear how all those women writhed and tore at your back and how they really didn't feel any more than I do."

"That shit-eating grin of yours! But tell me, what were they so excited about? I didn't know anything about fucking. You're the one who taught me about your friend down there. I just gave them the old in-out, in-out. Crude as hell, when you think about it."

Kate bounced onto him, her arms tight around his

neck. "I really do love you." She kissed his curls. "I just wish to hell I wasn't so fucking queer."

He stroked her back and quietly said that he'd rather watch her serve a tennis ball or come out of the water after a swim than make it with a moaning, groaning phony.

Horrified, Kate pushed him away.

"Now you're getting queer." He dismissed that possibility with a light wave of his hand. "Did it ever occur to you that this orgasm thing may be the biggest brainwash of them all?"

With growing anger, Kate listened to his theory that one pursued orgasms with the same ruthless ambition that marked any goal-centered activity. Having to have an orgasm was no different from having to win, he reasonably said, and involved the same fear of failure, which, if she thought about it, was the best sexual control that society could introduce. He kissed her gleefully. The claim that sexuality equals orgasm is as potent a damper on ordinary sensuality as the fear of unwanted children or the horror of the Catholic slow burn.

"That's a lot of shit!" On her knees, on the bed, in the dim room shouting: "I'm not into sex for the pleasures of children and seals. I want to open up, I want to feel!"

"You're feeling all the time, Kate, but you count it for nothing."

"You're just ducking the fact that we don't turn each other on. We never, never, never should have gotten married."

"Bullshit! The night of your – "

She smiled sarcastically. "Impalement?"

"No, no, no!" He looked at her stubbornly. "I was so

startled. Going to bed had been just a piece of cake and then, suddenly, there you were crying under the sheet, throwing up in the john. I'd never been moved by a woman before." He kissed her sweetly.

Kate surveyed him moodily. "I should love to know where you get the confidence to be so complimentary. Are you a saint?"

"I'm not charitable, you dumb cunt! I'm full of respect." He stared at her, his face growing hard. "You do turn me on." He swept her over.

"Let me get on top of you," she whispered.

"Hooray!"

Perched like a jockey on her husband's loins, the young woman looked down at her well-loved hands, saw them lose strength on the massive shoulders, saw them become the weak, white hands of a woman. As she began to ride, a strand of hair zapped up her nostril, then, in the space between their bodies, she saw the ignoble drag of male breast and stomach. Sneezing violently, she tumbled to the ground.

Breathless, fallen, she scrambled for any rock that came to hand. "You married me for my money."

An easy block for the handsome child of the sun. "Your money, honey, has great style, but I've got more of it."

Beat him now with a broken branch. "You're a social-climbing son of a bitch. You think my father's going to yank you into fame."

"The old gray men have had their day." Harry straddled her. "Would you kindly help me?"

Always the second time round, Kate began to feel,

then tense against the spreading warmth. It was the shitty truth that Harry was clean and bright while she festered, an old hag in a cave.

If the pleasure persisted, it darkly pleased her to run the reels of her sexual laboratory fantasy. In the city of her mean mind there existed Orgasms Unlimited, a commercial venture, run by a staff of blond, authoritarian Danes. In a huge room endless rows of both sexes were serviced in beds with crib sidings. Each bed was under the orbit of a hand, a soft, moist hand that hung from a metal arm.

The straightforward bureaucratic setting, the friendly, efficient hand calmed Kate's spleen. Once energized from the unseen control panel – all set, number 172! – the hand began its indifferent run, its light, unvarying touch divinely relentless.

No change of heart was acknowledged, one's arms and legs stayed comfortably bound until old hand had done its job. Useless to scream into the microphone, might as well cry out to Valhalla for all the good it did – person 172, kindly relax and enjoy.

Once ducked beneath one's sullen will, sensation was strong, peaking efficiently again and again, convulsing one to exhaustion on the multi-crested climax of an objective orgasm.

That Harry's arm was metal and his emotion electricity was Kate's secret, spitefully kept.

Harry softly kissed her face and neck, then lay on his back beside her. "Want an aspirin, honey?" She clenched her fists.

"For God's sake, why?"

"Your toe, dummy."

She sat up, shouting. "You're supposed to be dead outside the kitchen door. I was to have found my identity in notoriety, you rat."

Laughing softly, he dropped away. She curled against his back, a mood of humorless self-hatred hard in her chest. His strong, steady breathing moved her up and down.

"Harry?" She poked him meanly because she had nothing to say. He groaned patiently from a long way off, such a patient, tolerant groaning.

6

Elizabeth stepped in front of the painting lights, her shadow leaping over the platform where Kate and Margo stood talking. A Kleenex drifted from her hand; bending after, papers cascaded from her arms.

"Shit," she snarled, dropping to her knees, then violently sneezed.

Margo retrieved the Kleenex, shook it out, and passed it to Elizabeth, who glared at her from beneath her bangs.

"Why don't you stop pushing Kate to take off her clothes? She doesn't want to, so forget it." Margo gracefully extended her hand and pulled Elizabeth to her feet.

Kate sat down on the platform. Encircled by painting lamps, the two tall women confronted each other in a white pool of light. In the two loft windows behind, pigeons startled the blue glass. So bright, so fast, then gone.

Arriving back from her trip just an hour before, Elizabeth had been openly dubious at finding Kate in the loft. She did not in the least share Margo's enthusiasm about the portrait and for the first time in their friendship had shown herself as awkward and indecisive. She was going down to the law school, she'd say, then announce, as she cruised by the platform, that she'd decided to stay home and correct papers.

Now she stood solidly in her long tie-died robe, following Margo's flamboyant gestures with suspicious eyes.

"You must remember, darling, that when I'm painting, I'm never prurient."

"Liar!"

Margo ran her fingers through her hair, her eyes twinkling with pleasure. "You very wrongly think that of the two of us you are the only one capable of entertaining an idea."

Elizabeth graciously smiled. "Perhaps you've heard that there are some sensibilities so fine, no idea can penetrate them. Yours is one."

"You mean that as a supreme compliment, my love, but still, I must object. The process of painting is engrossingly concrete, yet, behind it, there is always an idea."

She stepped toward Kate on a long leg. "Sitting there as she is, all flesh and blood and shiny boots, your lovely cousin, for all her charming concreteness, is only interesting to me as an idea. An idea, I presume to think, that she's after in her own self. Why else would she go through a cancer operation at such a young age?"

"Such a fraud – " Elizabeth violently sneezed.

"My idea," (she paused while Elizabeth blew her nose), "my idea is that the figure presented should represent more than a modern mutilation, should give off, if I can do it, the excitement of myth."

"You just want to fuck her."

Margo challenged Elizabeth with bright, playful eyes. "How can you say that?"

"Kate's very attractive," Elizabeth fumed.

"She's extremely attractive, but she's housekeeping in the straight world."

"That's never stopped you before – you try to fuck all my friends."

"They all remind me of you." Margo charmingly shrugged. "I get carried away."

The calm of her broad brow half exposed by her dark bangs, Elizabeth ignored Margo's teasing expression. "I don't usually mind who you screw, but this time I do." She walked to the platform and put her arm around Kate. "In fact, if you make a pass at this one, I'll retaliate."

Margo thrust her hands in her pockets. Giving Elizabeth a fond, amused look, she pushed her pelvis forward. "You're being silly, darling. God knows we've talked and talked about it. The reason we're such a good team is that I'm interested in sex and you're not."

Elizabeth tossed her head, fiercely disgusted. "Margo Schwartz, you're believing in your own rules."

"My rules?"

"I'm just as interested in sex as you. You're just insanely jealous."

"Don't think I'm saying that you're not sexy." Margo shot her a heavy, approving look. "You are, you know – very. It's just that you don't have a sexual temperament except with me."

Elizabeth grinned at Kate. "You see, regardless of one's choice of gender, one can still end up with a chauvinist." She laughed incredulously. "Can you believe this?"

Margo smiled reasonably. "You know, I don't mind your being so naive."

"Of course, you don't mind, you ass, you created it." Margo shrank before the sudden bellowing force. "We were in bed two hours after we met. We spent one night together and decided to shack up, you decided. The second night was spent with your sea chest in the corner and resulted in your ultimatum divesting me of any sexuality except that directly stimulated by yourself. So far, I've been perfectly satisfied, but to find out that you really believe it – well, to hell with you!"

"But, darling, we've talked and talked about it. You have no sexual aura."

Elizabeth pushed her glittering face forward. "Then what attracted you?"

"Your delightful spirit."

"You're so smug in all your illusions, I really feel like telling you."

It was as if, between the two of them, there existed a law that no emotional state was ever lost, but simply transferred. For Elizabeth's mood was now light as helium while Margo sank like a stone. Her leg, as she crashed down on the platform, banged against Kate's like a wrecked door in the wind. She glowered up at Elizabeth's sparkling, flirtatious face.

"Tell me what, damn it."

"A very curious thing happened to me in Iowa."

"Ah, shit!"

Elizabeth smiled playfully. "All right, I won't tell you!"

"Tell me!"

Elizabeth took her time, striding regally, the hem of her long robe rippling subtly along the floor. Had Kate heard that Elizabeth had spent last week recruiting students for the law school? Wanting maximum contact with the girls – she smiled serenely at Margo – she'd asked to be put up in the dormitories of the various colleges she'd visited. One night, somewhere in Iowa, she woke up to find a very knowledgeable, hard-working chick in bed with her.

Margo stood up, threw wide her arms, and sat down. "Iowa," she agonized. "What did you do?"

Elizabeth's buoyant pleasure in the moment made Kate turn her head and smile. "It was very dark and at that point it seemed superfluous to ask her name – "

"How did you know it was a girl?" Margo croaked.

"Listen, my friend, I may have no sexual aura, but my tactile sense is acute and discriminate. Also, I'd forgotten my nightgown."

Margo clutched her head and pulled at her hair. "You were in that bed naked – Jesus, Elizabeth, I ought to smack you!"

Elizabeth stepped back with an injured look. "For losing my nightgown?"

Margo bowed her forehead to her knees. "What did you do?" she groaned.

"I did what any red-blooded, awake young American woman would do." Elizabeth flashed an apple-pie grin. "I rolled over and fucked her." She tapped Margo's gaunt cheek. "Isn't that what you would have done?"

She walked backward, laughing at Margo, who stalked her. "Well, isn't it?"

"Yeah, I would have done that, but you're not me."

Elizabeth fended her off, laughing delightedly. "I wanted to see what it was like being you. I must say, I rather liked it."

"I must say," Margo mocked. She grabbed for Elizabeth's neck. "Who was she?"

Elizabeth nodded gaily at Kate. "It was all very dark and extraordinary. All I can possibly tell you is that her breathing was lovely, that she smelled of Johnson's baby powder, and that she came with a bang, not a whimper."

Margo shoved Elizabeth against the platform and pinned her there, her large hands pushing against her shoulders and her hips shooting forward.

"I'm going to bang you, baby!"

"Ow! That hurts, Margo."

Margo bent down, lifted Elizabeth around the hips, plunked her on the painting platform beside Kate, and then flung herself on top, her face gaunt and wet with her amazing exertion. Panting, she bore down on Elizabeth with an open, mean mouth.

Elizabeth turned her head from side to side, as Margo tried to catch her lips. "Kate's here," she got out as Margo's hand clamped her chin.

"Kiss me!"

"I've got to go to work."

Margo moved lightly against Elizabeth's pelvis. "So let's work."

Elizabeth reached up, her hands pulling down Margo's dark, intense head as she jammed their mouths together. An instant later she broke away with a groan and hugged Margo hard.

"I did like being you."

"Well, don't ever be me again! I can't stand it."

She gustily kissed Margo's cheek. "You're adorably unfair."

"If you ever leave me, I'll die."

"Likewise," said Elizabeth, matter-of-factly. "Now

get off me and cool it till later. I have got to get back to work! Got to!"

It was decided in the kitchen over tea, the painting lights shut off for the while, that Margo, as usual, would have her way and that the portrait of Kate would be done without clothes.

The confident women smiled at whatever the other said and lighted each other's cigarettes. It was decided completely between the two of them, for the thought of standing without clothes on that bright, hot platform ducked Kate deep into anguished silence.

By the following Friday, the fourth time she'd unbuttoned her shirt and pulled off her jeans, Kate had not yet mastered the panic that struck when she must step out of the dimness into the blazing circle of light. Her arm came up and across her chest, her hand gripping her shoulder with a will of its own. This gesture was so awkward that she almost fell as she climbed the high step onto the platform. Margo would hold her very lightly, kiss her tense fingers, stroke her clamped arm, then work for a moment on her shoulders, which hiked up protectively when her arm finally dropped.

At the end of the first afternoon Margo made her a drink while she got into her clothes. As Kate came into the kitchen, Margo raised her glass and declared that Kate was the best model she'd ever had the pleasure to paint.

Kate politely smiled, drank, said nothing. The pain that shot through her body as she lumbered onto the platform was too intense to translate into Margo's blithe and breezy medium, and she could not have said why she felt more of a freak before Margo than before Harry or the handsome doctor who'd examined her a dozen times. Yet the hours of immobility under hot lights gradually buried the sensation of ugliness that flamed in her body and she felt herself drift slowly back until she floated free in a bright, warm sea.

When she finally heard Margo's "OK, love, that's it for today," Kate pulled softly up through the mildness and wincing, shivering, hit the cold place where the world chucked against her in hard, mean waves.

At night the pain in her legs and back would jump her out of sleep and Margo's intense, fluid gestures churned through her body. The stern look of her concentrating face, the dark wet of her chest, her sweat-flattened curls had made no felt impression on the model, but at night there hatched in Kate a clamorous yearning and it was no longer Valery St. John whose heat and hardness she wished to move against but the handsome lady painter.

As the bedroom moved up dim on all sides and the pain dulled in Kate's body, Margo, abstracted to shape and movement, would enter her and madly move. At dawn, Kate, done in by abstraction, dead tired of her own hand, would vow an end to the cowardly night-and-day duality of her post-adolescent life. She'd grind her teeth. At least kiss the woman, for crying out loud.

7

"For me, Kate?" Margo unwrapped the long, woolen scarf that the young woman had purchased at Bloomingdale's. Stretching it between her large, painty hands, she kicked the box under the kitchen table.

"It's an endless succession of red and white stripes, all knitted together." A tasseled end whirled round her neck; she stuck out a long leg, jutted her hip. "Thank you, my darling, Elizabeth will thrill to her gay, collegiate lover."

She sent the other end round her wet neck and put on the kettle. "I'm sick it's the weekend – where the hell is my brandy glass?" Kate picked a blue, drum-shaped thing out of the dish rack.

"That's it, thanks. It's going very well, you know. Better every day, which is why I hate to lose the momentum." Margo poured out her brandy – "You really are tough the way you hold that position. Most people collapse after twenty minutes but you go on and on." Margo raised her glass. "Well, cheers, Kate Stevens!"

She drank, then offered Kate the glass. Nips of brandy, puffs of grass were Margo's constant hospitality, which Kate kept turning down because the lights blinding her eyes and sucking the water from her skin were narcotic enough. Now she grabbed the glass from Margo's hand and knocked the brandy back.

Margo refilled the glass. At her amused look, Kate

dropped her eyes and stared fiendishly at the yellow linoleum. Margo's hand came quietly forward and raised her chin.

"I know you're all hung up, honey."

"I'm too ugly!" Kate blurted out.

Margo raised her brows.

"To live."

"You live very well." Margo kindly smiled.

"As an idea," Kate challenged.

"A very interesting idea. An idea that has a long life to live. I should like to keep my eye on that idea."

Kate concentrated on the glossy mass of white fridge, its bright edges. "You don't think I'm attractive."

Margo hitched up her broad shoulders and sighed. "Honey, I think you're the most adorable thing I've seen in years. I love you like a sister."

Kate yanked a paper towel from the rack, wet it, and pressed it against her eyes. "Just thanks," she grumbled.

"I never had a sister and I've always wanted one."

Savagely pressing the towel to her eyes, Kate croaked: "How do you feel about incest?"

Margo's eyes twinkled. "Incest?"

Kate packed the towel and shot it smartly into the waste basket at Margo's feet. An amused nod. "Not bad for a scamp."

"I want to go to bed with you as a political act."

"Kate, sweetheart, you're straight as a piece of string!"

"I have been – and I intend to get out of it."

"Why?" Margo coolly watched Kate's eyes flicking helplessly at her shoulders, breasts, and hips. She stretched cattishly as Kate explained that only a year ago she'd thought of homosexuality as a moral cop-out and a dangerous bypath that must be resisted in the name of growth.

"And what do you think now?

"Female homosexuality is a declaration of independence, no question about it!"

Margo waved an imaginary flag.

"You and Elizabeth are the first wave of a liberated society where the spirit of a person and not his or her gender will determine one's choice of a lover."

Margo beamed. "I'm a hero, not a pervert. I must write my mother, she'll be so pleased.

She slid down the gleaming white fridge, and her long legs bridged the yellow linoleum floor. Wedging her sandaled feet against the counter, she spoke through a violent yawn.

"Now, let me get this straight – excuse me, I'm shot – your message is that our sleeping together won't be lust or adultery, none of those boring bring-you-downs – it will be a political act."

"Exactly."

"Success, of course, depends on Elizabeth. If she can be brought to a correct understanding everything will be groovy." Margo winked. "Being so bloody political herself, I hardly suppose she'll be dense. Eventually, I suppose, we must all come to grips with the fact that fucking is political and therefore how absurd to be jealous. Makes sense."

Hands going deep in her pockets, Margo sharply beckoned with her head.

"Well, get on over here and start campaigning."

97

The young woman obediently straddled Margo's long, calm legs and delivered a kiss.

"Not on the cheek, my little ideologue." She took Kate's face between her hands and brought it to hers.

The softness of Margo's mouth, its quick flexibility, frightened Kate and she was glad when Margo slipped away from her and lay on the yellow floor.

"Well?" Her penciled brows arched wryly. Kate knelt in the yellow triangle made by Margo's legs.

"Get the radio," Margo commanded. "There, on the counter."

As Kate stood and reached for the small portable, a light, inward drizzle began. She watched Margo purposefully flick the dial to a relentless harangue of low chords and felt the hot flames of her fantasy fire grow tiny, go out. She knelt again as a victim.

Margo's strong hands slipped beneath Kate's arms and drew her up her body like a quilt. She undid her shirt and put Kate's hand on her breast. It lay there, too white and too small. Kate turned her head and conjured from the hard, white flank of the fridge the marble Margo who had so inflamed her imagination. Where was that bold, dark head that stood like a bust in Kate's nighttime solitude?

In her head the whiner started. This wasn't what it wanted at all; it really didn't want this at all. Kate slapped it down. Fuck the fridge then and shut up!

"I thought she'd be masterful, harder than steel. It isn't my fault," whined the whiner.

"Ah, Christ, you're rude. It isn't as though she's downstairs waiting. She's right under you."

"Damn you! Is she a beached whale?"

"She's so soft and quiet. It makes it all me – I hate me!"

"Then, be Harry! Find out what that's been like for the poor son of a bitch!"

Margo ran her hands down Kate's back and drummed softly on her ass. "Speech, speech," she whispered.

Kate kissed Margo's mouth, still alarmed at the softness of the woman's lips, the odd, light feeling of her head.

"Take my breast," Margo whispered, then quite fantastically lifted Kate in the air and set her down on the floor. "Elizabeth, damn it!" She sprang lithely to her feet, unwound the scarf from her neck, and spun it round Kate.

As Kate got herself upright and to the kitchen door, she was surprised to feel the wetness between her legs. The panic chute had been greased today, she'd had the fastest, coldest drop she'd ever survived, and yet, she was very noticeably wet.

Tall, calm, Elizabeth was reading the mail, with her raincoat collar dashingly up and a booted foot resting on her black briefcase. Margo sauntered up, slipped her hands beneath Elizabeth's coat, and quickly squeezed her breasts.

"Hard day at the front, my darling?" She took the letters from Elizabeth's hand and led her over to the painting.

"Well?"

Elizabeth looked briefly, picked a brush off the worktable, and drew with a flourish on Margo's open shirtfront.

"What?" Margo laughed.

"You get A for accomplishment. My, you get a great deal done in a day." Margo took the brush. "What else does the A stand for?"

"Hester in *The Scarlet Letter* was made to go about with a large, red A embroidered on her chest – remember?"

Margo shrugged. "I've read three books in my life, how would I know?"

With a swoop, Elizabeth braced Margo's head with her left hand and brought her right fist up to her nose. "I'm the knower, right? You, baby, are the feeler. Well, I want to tell you that I feel like shit."

Margo followed her into the kitchen, a small, pleased smile pulling at her lips. "You know it's never anything. We've talked about it."

Elizabeth turned in the doorway. "Right at the moment it doesn't particularly bother me that I can't get into my own kitchen for a cup of tea."

Kate shrank from Elizabeth's noble profile blaring past. A marvelous military back, putting on the kettle, getting down the cup. Side by side, Margo and Kate stared. When the steam whistled in the spout, Elizabeth turned around and pointed at Kate.

"Your husband is in terrible trouble and here you are" – she stamped the floor – "here you are carrying on. I don't care what you do with Margo – she's a professional child and it doesn't matter – but you're married to a great guy." Pushing back her bangs, the sudden whiteness of her fine brow was a hard rebuke.

"When Elizabeth gets mad her eyes gleam with blue fire," Margo said.

"I'm telling Kate that what she does with you doesn't matter because you're a professional child. But her husband isn't a child. He's in the middle of a terrible situation. He's got to think of nothing but that and here you are – " She pointed furiously at Kate. "What the fuck were you doing on my kitchen floor?"

Kate found a tea bag and poured the water into Elizabeth's cup. "What's the matter with Harry?"

"He's trying to keep that fool, Dean Bender, from calling the cops, he's under terrible pressure, and here you are, doing what, I'd like to know."

Kate's eyes slid away from Elizabeth's, then back. She held her cousin's disgusted gaze by counting the buttons on her tan lapel. "Why is Harry involved with the police?"

Elizabeth stared incredulously at Kate, then swept down on Margo and shook her by the shoulders. "Didn't you tell her what's going on? God, you're such a selfish baby!"

"Cut it out." Margo twisted away. "What's your problem? What do I know that I could have told?"

"It's been on the news all day."

Margo spread her arms imploringly. "What has been on the news all day?"

"Oh, stop! The radio's always on when you work."

"Not always, baby! Not today."

"Not today, huh?" She struck at Margo, who blocked her hand and held it. "While you were seducing this child, her husband was battling for his life – still is."

"I'm not a child!" Kate protested.

"I don't give a shit about her husband!"

"Great – just great!" Kate tugged at Elizabeth's sleeve, poked her arm, then, in desperation, picked up the tiny transistor radio and raced the dial around.

"Margo Schwartz, you're so incredibly narrow. There's a whole world out there where things are

101

happening, Today there was a real political thing – her husband's in the middle of it – the only white man who has a clue to what's going on – and look at you cloistered in this loft, painting, turning on, but really turning off to what's actually happening. Do you know what's happening?"

Margo opened her mouth and closed it, then laid her head on her arm as though exhausted.

"We're in the middle of a revolution – something much, much bigger than your so-called art. Harry Stevens knows what really happened. He's a great person; he's really trying where it counts. He's not smoking pot and boozing and fucking all day on kitchen floors."

On her arm, Margo cruised her fingers over her scalp and softly groaned. "You know I said nothing about Harry Stevens as a person. If he's the saint you say he is, I'm glad of it. I only remarked that I didn't give a shit about Kate's husband."

"Oh, don't mind me, by the way, girls - I'll just listen to my radio ..."

"Stop trying to slide out, Margo. You hate men. You have a fanatical hatred of men."

A long, painty finger rose from her curls. "Husbands, not men – a distinction even a lawyer should see."

Elizabeth bent over, her pale eyes glittering close to Margo's curls. Her mouth, in profile, drew a bitter, downward line. "That's an insanely arbitrary distinction. Men are husbands and husbands are men and your saying otherwise shows that your childish ambition to become a man has finally flipped you out."

Sitting up, Margo took Elizabeth's intense face between her hands and teasingly kissed her lips. "I don't want to be a man anymore than I want to be a woman." She gestured at Kate. "We're all the same here; we're all new. Look at our friend, perched up there on the counter, with the radio pressed to her ear. She's cute as hell. I think of what she could have been if she hadn't jumped into the marriage box and slammed down the lid, and yes, I do hate her husband because, as her husband, he can only stand in her way."

Elizabeth smiled cruelly. "Do you really think Kate would leave Harry Stevens for you?"

"She'd be a fool not to."

"But you're just a poor, sad, homosexual woman and he's a king."

Margo patiently shook her head. "You don't get the picture, honey. Kate comes down to us because we're strong and free. Freaks, yes, but strong, good freaks. If she's got the guts to stick around, she'll learn a lot."

Elizabeth crowed. "What could she possibly learn from you?"

"Just what you learned, pal, when you first came to me."

"I didn't come to you."

"At the Voyager, you marched right up to me." She tried to kiss Elizabeth's hand. "You were bold as brass."

"You were drunk."

"Strategically drunk. I wanted to see how far you'd go. Far and fast. I was in bed before I knew what hit me."

"I wanted to find out."

"That you were marvelous!"

"Oh, crap!"

"You're shit, right? And Harry Stevens is a king."

"He's responsible for the African American program at the law school. He's pushed it like Hercules and now, the way the faculty is reacting, the thing may slide back and crush him."

"You go around the country recruiting females for the law school – that's never been done before."

"There's so much wrong with us." Elizabeth glowed with a malignant triumph. "We're lesbians!"

Margo looked at her with cool disgust. "I'm me, thank god. I'm immunized."

Elizabeth hated her. "Against what?"

Margo's long finger pointed silently at her, then she turned, picked a glass from the cupboard and poured herself a small brandy. Elizabeth walked round the table, pulled out a chair, and sat down opposite Margo, whom she regarded steadily with lethal eyes. Margo didn't flinch.

"Tell me about the revolution, darling."

Elizabeth picked up the brandy bottle. "Christ, Margo, that was full a day ago!"

"That was a day ago." Margo smiled sweetly at her own rationality. "Now, tell me all about Harry Hero and his doings."

"I could kill you, Margo."

"All this striding up and down the front lines has made you tense and irritable. Take off your coat and have a drink."

"I will!" Elizabeth shouted and Margo got up and fetched two glasses as though directed by the sweetest request in the world. She poured out two drinks and passed one to Kate.

"You keep forgetting that I'm the one that's married

to Sir Harry! Tell me the news, for God's sake, and let me drink my brandy in peace."

Kate tried to sit more alertly on the counter. Elizabeth turned in her chair, her angry eyes sliding away from Kate's face and settling on her muffled neck.

"What is that?" She pointed.

Kate looked down at the ridiculous red and white tassels and furtively scratched her neck as Margo explained that just a few hours ago she'd received the scarf as a gift from Kate.

The dismay in her cousin's face shocked Kate. Her arms shot out to comfort, then hung awkwardly.

"Are you in love with her?" Elizabeth's social advantage, the heavy weapon that she was heir to, but that Kate had never known her to use, flew into her hand and she struck.

A soft, dark, sagging sound came out of Margo. Then she dug her hand into her curls and pulled her head up, yelling: "There's the prejudice!"

"Yes, yes, yes!" Elizabeth hurled her brandy glass. Kate screamed as a drop of blood crept from Margo's scalp and trickled down her forehead.

"It's the nobodies like you who ruin everything! The students took over Fayerweather Hall today in a peaceful protest at the murder of James Eaton and now it's all finished because some nobody secretary had to fall down the stairs!" Margo's hand flew up, frightened and warding. "She's going to die, damn it! Abd we're all pitched out! Pitched out!"

Margo looked numbly at the paper towel that Kate put into her hand, then pressed it matter-of-factly to her brow and finished off her brandy. Kate reached over her shoulder for the bottle and poured her another. The tasseled end of the scarf slipped into the glass.

"Will you take that *thing* off?" Elizabeth shouted.

"Yes, do, darling," Margo dully said as she regarded the bloody towel in her hand.

Kate looked disgustedly at the sodden wool. She rolled it into a neat cylinder and shoved it under the heavy wooden frame of the kitchen window, which was open a crack. An absurd thing to have bought for Margo!

"I cut you!" Elizabeth's voice was aggressive but her eyes hopped furtively along the wall above Margo's head. "I threw that glass and I cut you!"

"A scrape, you stupid bitch! A two-year-old could have drawn more blood." She flicked the bloody towel across the table onto Elizabeth's shoulder. The horrified urgency of Elizabeth as she dashed the towel off made Margo laugh bitterly. "Not blue enough for you, hey? Sorry about that!"

"Oh, shit!" Elizabeth shouted at the ceiling.

"Elizabeth," said Kate. "You were telling us about the students taking over Fayerweather Hall. Can you at least go on?"

Elizabeth turned her eyes from Margo's sardonic face. In a childish, apologetic voice she told how she and Harry had been sent into the building at the request of the black students, so that they might relay their demands to Dean Bender.

"What about the demands of the girl who 'fell' down the stairs?"

"She did fall, Margo," Elizabeth humbly asserted.

106

"Pushed, thrown down the stairwell, stumbled over her own feet – you could care less! And all those male students could care less! You talk about me being drugged up! Jesus, Liz, politics is the biggest, phoniest high of all."

"It was all Dean Bender's fault," observed Kate quietly.

"We were inside, talking to the guys, and suddenly there was this hideous shriek of sirens, then doors slamming and voices coming over megaphones. There were swarms of police on the lawn, half of them wearing gas masks, all of them carrying billy clubs. It was terrifying!"

The corners of Elizabeth's mouth glistened with saliva as her small voice recited the nightmare scene. She stared at Margo, her eyes huge and trusting.

"That's when the girl got it?"

Elizabeth shook her head. "That's when *we* got it! Willy Hay shouted that Harry had double-crossed them. He was really mad, and I don't blame him. But then – " she flailed, emotional. "Then four of them held Harry down and they beat him – Willy kicked him in the genitals ... "

Offering her final apology to Margo, her hand pulling at her collar, Elizabeth said: "They hit me, too."

Margo leaned across the table. Kate stared over her shoulder, as her cautious fingers discovered the ripped front of Elizabeth's dress and a bruise beneath.

"Those creeps," Margo murmured. "What a bunch of creeps!"

Elizabeth reached into her coat pocket and showed them a plastic vial filled with shiny red pills. "I got painkillers at the infirmary," she said, smiling wryly at Kate. "Harry got some too, but his are blue. We both got checked for broken bones and internal damage and we're both fine, except for the bruises. Harry must be home by now."

Kate's jacket was at the end of the loft, lying on the steps of the painting platform. On her way to the iron door, she passed by the bathroom on quiet feet and saw Elizabeth sitting on the edge of the bathtub, her head bowed and arms outstretched as Margo drew off her dress. The sudden white gleam of her back made Kate feel like a spy and she sped away, hauling on her jacket, while her boots tapped an alacritous rhythm from the wooden stairs.

8

Kate Stevens stood with her back to the bed where her husband slept. She wore a nursing costume of her own devising, having added a white cotton shirt to the jeans that she'd worn all day. She'd scrubbed her fingernails and filed them to an appearance of nurse-like competence, sternly brushed back her dark hair, and polished up her boots. She now hung out of the window, looking at the full moon.

Valery St John's cheekbones tingled as she watched bright clouds sail north down the corridor of roofs. Once she'd walked across the top of the world, down Canada and onto the high, dry back of America, drowning bodies in the stream of time, her bones holding beneath her fluid, changing skin, from white to red to white again.

Hard against the mountains, she'd practiced life and death, just wizardry, just grace, the persistent reappearance of that wild face, then down the bounding rivers, past settlements, villages, jubilant towns to the edge of the sea where towers raced each other up the violent air.

"Hey, Luna," she called, "this is my current address." Ducking in, she slipped on her bright boots and strode a bit in this particular place. Green rug, blue walls, a huge bed where a warrior lay, self-crowned in bright hair – so big he was, his limbs hung out in space, all bruised.

Beside the door a wooden valet held his large suit

silently and his Rose Bowl cufflinks and his vast shoes. A bottle of Scotch stood at his head, while his thick books, folders, and yellow pads spread out from his calloused feet, a patient archipelago. "Sweet lord, sleep," they cried.

Back and forth, back and forth, the young woman delighted to spring herself to life each time she passed the long mirror on the bathroom door. She paused, a hand on her cowboy hip. Tall and lean, the hardest pelvis this side of the divide. Whenever she moved on Margo, that hard-faced lady had groaned so softly from her subtle mouth.

The young woman stiffened, bravely confronting her image. A bitter yellow voice had just kicked open the door of her pleasant front mind, pulled up the softest chair and sprawled.

It said: "You just want to eat pussy."

"Sure thing!" She was Valery St. John, after all. She'd lived for thousands of years and couldn't be more perfect. She was a fat idea with lots of tread.

"You want to fuck the shit out of that decadent woman, don't you."

"Up one leg and down the other! Hip, hip, hooray!"

"You'd really like to fuck her with your boots on. You'd like to split her in two with your long rod."

"Fuck, fuck, fuck, fuck! Eyes, ears, nose, and throat. Breast, tit, cunt, toe."

The voice armed up with irony and social pride. It crossed its legs, wearing golden evening slippers and a highborn face.

"It isn't totally unimaginable to me how you could sleep with her, but to be seen on the streets, in broad daylight, holding her hand?"

Valery grinned. "Oh, Mother, I know it's you. Don't be jealous. I want to fuck you too."

"That, I *can* understand." The voice composed itself for a sulk. "I suppose one must do all sorts of ingenious things to make up for the boring similarities. However, the best cuisines are founded on bland meat."

Cheerfully, Valery waved good-bye. She turned from the mirror and sat on the bed between Harry's legs. Legs, groin, stomach, and chest all carried heavy bruises. At the end of his thick man's neck bloomed a sweet face; beneath the bright curls, inside the skull, was a hurt mind.

She'd taken the subway home from the Chinatown loft. Climbing the dim stairs, she'd seen Harry climbing ahead of her, his two hands on the orange railing hauling so slowly that a crowd blocked up behind him, restless and rude.

Kate stepped onto the street and called his name. He didn't hear her. People swerved past him, their faces angry and frightened as they looked up. "Drunken bum," a small woman sneered. Harry's head turned slowly around. Kate froze in the dense evening crowd, then was jostled against the fender of a parked car. Her horrified impression that Harry had been blinded turned out to be the fact that he'd lost his glasses.

Usually his fast, buoyant stride made her run and the upward tilt of his head flashed clouds across his round glasses and darts of sun. Now he crawled with a face of clay.

Harry stepped off the curb, the red streetlight shining over his head. "Wait," Kate cried. A delivery boy, his white jacket belled in the wind of his speed, bicycled down on

Harry, the huge wire basket filled with boxes aimed at his hip. Barely turning his head, Harry shot out his hand and caught the rim of the basket, stopping the bicycle and catapulting the young black kid through the handlebars into his arms. He stared for a moment at the terrified face, then vindictively hurled the boy into the overturned boxes and strewn food.

His violence and large, lurching body momentarily stymied reaction and he'd turned off the avenue before the mild outcry began. The boy was lifted and examined, the groceries put back on the bike, and a policeman finally arrived. Did anyone know which way the fellow had gone?

"I'm pretty sure I saw him step into that liquor store."

No, no, no! A chorus of voices contradicted her. He'd turned left at the corner. Kate hurried off. Fortunately, the street where she lived was clear.

Nicholas, the night elevator man, laughed about Mr. Stevens coming home in the bag. They didn't make them any better, though, Kate could be sure of that.

The elevator door slammed shut. Kate gasped to see Harry standing like a statue in front of their door. His dull face slowly turned to her.

"No key," he croaked.

Behind the closed kitchen door, Cam was crowing and Mrs. Quinn was on the phone. Kate led Harry through the living room and down the hall to their bedroom. He hung onto the high bureau while she took off his jacket, his tie, and his belt. She knelt and untied his shoes, dredged the empty bottle from his back pocket, and went for more Scotch.

When she told him that Mrs. Quinn had said he was a hero, he beamed up at her from his pillow and then burst into tears.

"I thought Willy Hay was my friend, Kate. I really trusted him. I - I just assumed that he trusted me."

"I know," said Kate, holding his hand.

"He even knew that! When he smashed my glasses with his foot, he said, 'Don't look at me with those hurt eyes, man!' I mean, what is that?"

"I don't know. It's all nuts."

Finally, the painkiller, the Scotch, and the violent crying put Harry into a deep sleep.

Elizabeth called to find out about him and told Kate that Harry Stevens was a magnificent person. Rust in Kate's eyes and throat! Elizabeth would never say that about her!

But, why not? Why slink to the back of her cave and lie among bones? Kate Stevens was no longer living alone. At this moment of her life she was rooming with Valery St. John and could wear her boots any time she liked.

Kate poured Scotch into the water glass and called her only childhood friend. Tony Butler had nested in northern California and announced the hatching of her children by printed card. Was it earlier or later in California by the sea? She dialed and dialed because it was late for them both. Damn! Picked up by Tony's husband, a Rotary Club basketball player with wildly long arms.

"Hi! This is an old friend of Tony's. I've just had the most marvelous baby. Tony must know." Valery waited, gulping Scotch. Then her friend came on the line.

"Tony, old bean! Where are you in time and space?

Indeed, I have! A baby as beautiful as the sun. I have them often, but this one sprang full grown from my brow, like Athena. I've named her Valery and she's going to change our lives ... "

"Certainly, I'm drunk. Harry's been in a fight and I'm nursing him. He's bound to wake at any moment and then I shall have to hang up and tend to him tenderly. Every four hours I tenderly tend and, in between, I drink."

"Tony, baby, do you remember when we used to throw tennis balls against the side of your garage? I loved that, did you? Remember all the money we stole out of your mother's purse? Six movies a weekend in our prime. Do you know what I've been thinking, Tony? You know, all that time, we should have been with each other. Relax, hon, you're in the sunshine state and I'm a resident of Gotham. Do you smoke? Well, then, get a cigarette. Listen, when you were ten, you were terrific, the toughest, darkest thing – hair, eyes, and spirit. David Tabor crumpled me up in the school yard and you were furious. We got him good the next day. We were a team!"

"I miss you! I saw a child that looked like you in the park. I wanted to tag after her and cry and cry. I wish we hadn't been so hands-offish. I can't understand it. There we were, hour after hour, frying in our own lust. Certainly, get some juice, get a cookie too."

Valery winked down at Harry's peaceful face, then laid her clean, competent fingers on his pulse. "There you are, Tony. What's all the shouting about? Chambers is your husband, right? He wants to go back to sleep? But I called especially to wake him up.

"Butler, you're stupid about men! You watched while

Billy Bird threw me out of your house. We were listening to the Brandenburg Concertos, which you switched off when you saw his car and put on some shit! Glen Miller, I think. Damn right, I'm still mad. Mad as hell! We were like sisters, we were a team and then big, dumb Billy Bird clunked into your life – he tossed me over the railing of your front porch – and you let him!"

"You felt so superior because you'd finally gotten a boyfriend. Then I put on the dog because I got a better boyfriend. Too awful!"

"Is that Chambers I hear? Tell him to go out into the sunshine and dribble up his ass! Hold it, hon, one second more for the message. Hey, my long-lost friend, don't sell out your daughter. It is imperative that we do not sell out our daughters. OK? Signing off, sweetheart. Squeeze a glass of juice for me."

Valery took off her jeans, closed the closet door on her boots. It was four hours to the minute when Harry groaned and Kate Stevens stood by with a painkiller in her hand and a glass of water all ready to go.

9

As the iron bolt of the loft door slid back Kate assumed a casual position in the hall. It jolted her to hear Elizabeth's voice. Every other morning she'd found Margo alone.

In the margin of the opening door Margo was walking away. She waved.

"Come on in, we're fighting."

Kate followed Margo's tall, retreating figure dressed in blue. As she went, the huge eye of Margo's self-portrait caught light from the circle of painting lamps and glowed like a small sun.

"Here's our girl!" Mounted on the high kitchen stool, one shapely leg looming in the slit of her housecoat, Elizabeth welcomed Kate with generous arms. Her neck feathered against Kate's face, the skin feeling younger than Margo's and unalert.

"How is Harry this morning?"

"He got out of bed and went down to the law school to have lunch with Dean Bender. He took two painkillers and stumbled out."

Margo drummed her fingers on the table and looked cynical. Elizabeth glared over the coffeepot and cups.

"Do you hear what Kate is saying, Margo? She is saying that Harry Stevens is so involved that even though he's more dead than alive, he's down at the law school doing his job."

Margo cheered softly through her hands. "Hooray!"

Elizabeth's mouth grew mean, her pale eyes gleamed.

"So selfish, so narrow-minded, so absurdly prejudiced against men that she can't even see how great your husband is – let alone admit to it." She tossed her head. "Get yourself some coffee, coz."

Gratefully, Kate moved to the stove and kept her back to both of them.

"I told you I was impressed with the man. I think he's absolutely terrific, tough as nails, a hero, in fact."

"That's not at all what you said," Elizabeth fumed. "You said to me, five minutes before Kate knocked on the door, that Harry Stevens was acting in his own interests."

Margo sighed. "Kate, darling, isn't it true that Harry comes in when and if the present dean goes out?"

"Why do you lie to Kate? – what you actually said was, 'Old bums out, new bums in.'"

Margo stepped behind Kate and laid her hands casually on her shoulders. "Finish your coffee, hon. To work! Christ, it's late."

Elizabeth spun round on the stool, saying over her shoulder: "You think painting is the most important thing in the world."

"Lizzy baby, much more than my work, what matters to me is you, is us, is our relationship. You can't say that – so get off your high horse.

Kate sat down on the platform and slowly took off her boots and socks. The lights burned down. As they argued, Kate watched Elizabeth's vigorous nipples beneath her pink robe; the gold in Margo's teeth.

Pacing majestically, Elizabeth grew short of breath

and began to pant. "You want me to stay home all day so that I can cook your lunch."

"You have no classes until four on Monday, right?" She waved a weary hand at Elizabeth's stubborn, glittering face.

In a dead, righteous tone, Elizabeth said, "Of course I have to go to the law school today."

Casually adjusting a lamp, Margo asked: "What are you going to do with yourself, pick up the lawn?"

The heavy pink skirt dragged back and forth, Elizabeth's knees solemnly poking through the opening. "So damned amusing, you think you are. Pick up the lawn! Do you know what I'm really going to do? I'm going to ask every student I see how he feels about the administration calling in the cops and if they're disgusted enough to put their names to a petition demanding the resignation of Dean Bender."

Margo was stunned. "Honey, baby, do that and you're going to be eating your lunch home every day."

Elizabeth's stern arms folded down over her bosom, ending reverie. "You think that nothing exists in the world but your activity with a paintbrush. Well, I'm involved in activity too – political activity – and when I go out this door, all I can tell you is I don't know when I'll be home."

Old in the eye and mouth, Elizabeth stared at the painting. Margo swept up, her long arm going about Elizabeth's waist.

"More than anything, I care about our day-to-day life. Everything else is phantoms."

"You've gotten tired, Margo, you accept the way things are." Elizabeth stepped away. "I won't be like that."

"Hey – I'm a woman *born* to the battle – damn right, I'm tired. I'm forty-one and I really don't give a shit anymore, except for you." She made a wry face. "You, who are against all the brooding, personal people, who think that nothing in the world is so beautifully self-justifying as a crisp, executive order."

"You think that all political activity is worthless."

"We're two women trying to make it in a man's world and that's as political as you can get."

"It's a death box here." Elizabeth rolled her eyes toward the door. "I will never again live with another woman!"

Margo looked insolently at Elizabeth's nipples. "You're not just passing through, you know."

Elizabeth blushed violently. "You're just a stage, damn you! If I lived minute to minute inside these walls – if I had to think that your painting was everything, I'd go crazy!"

"You are crazy!" Margo turned her back. "Now, go away!"

Elizabeth hung about, tried to take Margo's hand. "We're two women living together, Margo. We can't just huddle together. We've got to make our mark."

"Uptight, WASP bitch!" Margo pushed her away. "Don't know you have a body, don't taste your food or relish your sleep."

"I love to drink." Elizabeth ironically smiled.

"Because the liquor goes straight to your head and feeds your idea. You're a militant child of Christ barging into other people's battles and knocking them right and left with your damned cross."

"There are real battles to be fought. I don't make them up."

"You should whittle down that cross, baby, and swallow it. Then you'll know where the battle is."

Elizabeth gazed humorously at Kate. "She thinks I'm neurotic."

"What the hell would you call it? A day at home, leading a normal life with me, and you begin to fester. It's pathetic."

"I don't think it's normal to smoke pot all day and fuck around," Elizabeth cried defensively. "At age forty-one that's pathetic."

"At least it's an attempt to get out. The mind is no exit, baby, the mind is a maze." Margo tapped her forehead. "God, it's been so painful in here. I used to get terrible headaches, one morning I woke with a whopper and I thought, Christ, I've been invaded. Of course, I had, but I didn't realize that it had happened years ago. Happened when I was born. Babies are uninhabited countries, you know, and then strange hordes pour through the mountain passes. They build a city, fortify it, and then start working on the surrounding countryside."

Her hand drew a quick line from her chin to her belt buckle. "They tell you how to think and what to feel. If you fall short or wide of their miserable directions they tell you to go out and beat your head against the wall – because it's your fault. I was obedient for years, carefully listening, trying hard to obey – and look at the expression on my face!" She jabbed her thumb at her self-portrait.

"That poor, bullied, miserable thing. Beneath the smile, of course. I'm a subtle painter." She smiled boldly at Elizabeth. "You think I'm frivolous for smoking pot, for trying to feel, but I'm running from wolves." She flung wide her arms. "A pack of ravening wolves."

Elizabeth looked attentively at Margo long after she'd finished speaking. She shyly reached out, her fingers barely grazing Margo's arm, then they closed in a fist that she pounded on her leg.

"Inside is all right for you, fine for you, but don't you see that one of us has to be out? To see what it takes to be out? One of us has got to learn from men."

"Are you dumb! What more can you learn? They don't care about you! They don't care about the girl they threw down the stairs!"

Elizabeth moved her shoulders and head as though invisible hands had dropped a net over her and drawn it tight. "Really, Margo, I think about you all the time out there."

She walked away, clumsily unzipping her long, pink wrapper. "I just got to go!"

Margo strode to the edge of the lights, bellowing: "Go, then! Get your brains beaten out! I don't care!" She hove past Kate. "Are you going too? Is that why you've got every damned strip of clothing on?" Her dark face meanly loomed.

"Well?" Margo didn't look around as Kate lumbered up on the two steps of the platform. She slipped her feet into the footmarks pressed into the felt covering by the two weeks of posing and darkened by sweat.

The loft door slammed. Margo held the paintbrush like a sword as she came at the canvas. "Your left foot looks like a bladder."

Kate looked anxiously down.

"This foot, silly." Margo jabbed at the canvas with the brush, then stepped back and with an agonized look and flung the brush at her feet.

"Caught out at last," she cried. "No shirt on my back, can't paint, never could. My activity with a paintbrush – ?" With a swoop, she picked up the brush and obscenely saluted the painting.

"Get dressed, will you? I'm going to cut my throat."

She turned off the painting lights, leaving Kate to get dressed in the semi-dark. The fridge door opened and closed, and the ice tray banged on the counter.

The squeal of bed springs caused Kate's scalp to tingle and when she'd picked her way between the standing lamps and taken the brass bedpost in her hand, Margo was sipping a black drink, her legs flung over the bed in despair.

An old-fashioned brass bedstead covered with a yellow chintz quilt. Elizabeth's pink housecoat hung from a hook beside the bed; two small un-painted bureaus stood on either side.

"It looks like boarding school," Kate said.

Margo laughed. "Elizabeth to the left, myself to the right, but not really." She drank and offered the glass to Kate.

"Why are you refusing?"

"I don't like to drink in the afternoon."

"Why not?"

Kate wanted to be light. "If you drink before six you turn into a white rabbit."

Margo belched. "Turn out of one, you mean." A black smile. "You and Elizabeth are just alike. Jesus!" She sat up and aggressively held out the glass. Kate took a tiny mouthful and passed it back.

"Tell me why?" Margo asked.

"Why what?"

"Why you don't drink in the daytime."

"I think I have an addictive personality."

"Of course, you do." Her large hand patted the quilt. "I hate to see a sweet, young chick looming over me. Sit, please. I'm much too down to make a pass. Ah, look how gingerly she sets herself down. You and Elizabeth are twins. Tell me the difference between shrews and human beings?"

"Aren't shrews the animals that eat every twenty minutes?"

"Indeed they are." Margo ran her hand through her hair. "How often do you eat?"

Kate thought. "Every five or six hours."

"The shrew eats every twenty minutes and you eat approximately every three hundred minutes. Now, tell me this. Are you more or less addicted to food than the shrew?"

"Less. No, more! The same, obviously."

"Of course. All living things are addicted to food, to air, to water, to sleep. Elizabeth can't bear that fact. I suppose you can't either, so the two of you spend all your time worrying about your addiction, thinking that your fierce controls change the nature of the dependence, which they do not."

"You must control yourself."

Margo turned on her side and regarded Kate pleasantly. "Why? We've achieved a certain low civilization

123

– all the tough organizing stuff is done, at least in this part of the world. Food is distributed, clothes are available, and there is access to money. When it's wet, one can be dry, and warm, if one wants, when it's cold. All that glorious stuff is done, all that nose-to-the-grindstone necessary stuff of our grandparents and parents – just finished. We're all standing on a marvelous foundation and we have to learn to fly."

She drank some more, then sat up and bent her forehead to her knees. "I'm still on the ground. I can't believe I'm safe. I still paint like a businessman. I'm a rigid, competitive, success-mad fuck."

Everywhere but her face, Margo's skin was smooth and tight, as if pulled by pegs, and sweetly dark. Kate looked at the line of her shoulders and back under the blue work shirt. Her face wanted to feel this skin through the cotton, her hands wanted to touch.

"Do you know that after years and years of trying to crack the case, after booze and pot and sex, sex, sex, I still stand in front of a canvas as though at an inquisition?" Margo looked up plaintively. "My so-called activity with a paintbrush fills me with guilt. The way in is the way out, they say, and I'm in, I think, but spinning. Elizabeth rushes out into the street, while I spin myself into nausea, praying for tread." She smiled tensely at Kate. "Pretty soon I'll be a speck at the bottom of my ditch. My head will look no larger than a beetle."

Shyly, Kate stroked Margo's head. "Nice head," she croaked. A hurricane in a pale balloon. Oh, God, she would burst, she would die!

Margo looked up from her knees and playfully patted

Kate's leg. "Still interested in politics, are you?" In the warmth of Margo's scalp Kate's hand burned, but the rest of her was cold.

Margo lay back. Her elbows spiked as her hands went behind her head. She looked wryly at Kate from the corner of her eye. "Have you ever been with a woman?"

"No."

Margo got up. "Come on," she beckoned. She took the glass of Scotch a few feet beyond the partition to the rim of a large red rug.

"I need space," she smiled. She smelled under her arms. "Need a bath, too."

Switching off one lamp, turning on another, going for her weed rolled tight in a plastic bag, then her cigarette papers, which she kept in her purse, Margo softly hummed while her hips rode the waves of her motion. Kate sat cross-legged on the red rug, her eyes glued to Margo's supple form. Fearful. Full of fear. Never more so than now. Kate listened to the shower water, looked at the cigarette papers half buried in the thick, red rug. Roll some joints, Margo had commanded, swinging off.

Fully clothed, head bowed, Kate sat and sat on cold, cramped legs.

A cloud of strong, spicy perfume preceded Margo from the bathroom. Kate picked up the papers, picked up the bag, held them out to Margo, who suddenly loomed on top of long, brown legs. "I don't know how to roll joints," she said.

A yellow shirt, soft and flying around her torso. Black bikini underpants. "Neither does Elizabeth, although she smokes them, you bet."

Sitting down on the rug, Margo instructed her. One of her thumbs was misshapen, very wide and squat, the thumbnail half split and the skin of the tip parted in a deep crack. It looked so painful that Kate touched it, asking why she didn't cover it with a Band-Aid.

"Looks god-awful. Doesn't hurt, though." Margo creased the cigarette papers – she used two – licked the gummed edges, then tapped the green shreds into the crevice. "My brother smashed my thumb years ago. 'Hold it out,' he said, and I did – smash! It doesn't have any feeling, which is why." She held out the joint: "This is such a mess."

She lit up, inhaled, and passed it to Kate.

"You'd never believe I've been rolling these things for twenty years."

Kate held the smoke against a cough, inhaled a few more times, and then dared to look frankly at Margo.

Lovely, lovely weed, transforming fear to joy!

"Don't you just love this?" Kate asked.

The lady tipped back her head, smiled with amused surprise, then glided down and put her head in Kate's lap.

"You're cute as they come," Margo said.

The head's smallness, its frail weight on Kate's leg, changed her mood from joy to panic. The sight of her own hand stroking Margo's forehead and hair repelled her and she reached out with the other and grabbed the metal arm of the couch. "Oh, most enviable properties,' she thought, 'enter me!"

Thought but not heard above the roar of the storm that raged within her. Head into the wind, she told herself, ride it through, for behind the fear she recognized the hard desire waiting to be served. Kate bent her face over Margo's and kissed her mouth. She searched Margo's lips, her tongue, and teeth for the force that was in her gestures, in her talk. Why didn't Margo kiss her back? Put her arms around her. Why did she lie like the dead?

Kate slammed down on her then, slammed that bright cold knot of desire against Margo's pelvis. She heard herself panting, felt her body tremble.

"Yes, yes, yes," Margo moaned from some deep, narcotic place and the sound, the dim, languorous, passive sound, infuriated Kate and she drove against Margo, biting her neck, sucking her soft lower lip into her mouth, wanting to split Margo open, wanting to kill her.

"Go easy, hon."

She unbuttoned Margo's shirt. Her breasts lay leisurely against her bony chest. Margo raised her chest impatiently to Kate's mouth. "Take the whole thing," she demanded.

As her mouth drew in Margo's breast, Kate's desire separated itself from fear and grew stronger, finally dominant. Margo's nipple grew hard in her mouth and she pressed it urgently with the back of her throat. Her hand shot beneath the band of Margo's black bikini, past the ridge where she always found herself, and into the woman, as far as she could go.

Loving the heat, the smoothness, the sweet clamp of skin and muscles round her fingers, Kate could rest there for a thousand years! Rest and rest!

"Take your hand away, darling!"

"No!"

Margo laughed. "Just for a second."

The grip Margo had on her hand delighted Kate. She could feel her clitoris on her wrist and as Margo raised her hips and kicked her pants over both their heads, Kate moved her wrist softly.

Margo gave Kate a curt, congratulatory nod. "You didn't miss a beat."

"I love this!" Kate laughed. "I really, really do."

"Darling girl, my most darling girl, go down on me, please."

Her wide, split, tortured thumb plucked at herself and gave Kate a piece of dark tissue to suck. In an instant, fear and revulsion were again corralled behind her breastbone and pushing out her breath. She closed her eyes as her tongue reluctantly touched.

"Oh, lovely," Margo groaned, raising her hips and moving delicately against Kate's mouth. Her fingers pressed Kate's neck and pinched her ears. A low sound came with her quickened breath.

Kate loved her light motions, the sound she made. She loved her taste, the taste of a tough and cunning guerrilla fighter, who patiently, through the years, was reclaiming herself, bit by bloody bit.

Margo dug her fingers into Kate's hair and pulled.

"You do that beautifully ..."

Margo's stomach trembled beneath Kate's hands, her thighs closed round her head and rocked her urgently while Kate held and held.

"Enough, oh, Christ, enough!"

Reluctantly, Kate slid up Margo, drying her face on her beating stomach.

"I love you, I love you! Boy, do I love you!"

The loved lady yawned and stretched. "I must say that was a very creditable maiden voyage." She kissed Kate affectionately on the forehead. "What a very pleasant surprise."

Margo stretched back for her pants. "You've the most beautiful back," Kate said. "You're so strong."

Margo smiled kindly. "You're not bad yourself, kiddo."

She walked to the bed and pulled on her jeans. A long arm flew up the yellow sleeve of her shirt. "I think I know what I've been doing wrong with that foot – come on!"

Kate followed her, unbelieving. "Are we going right back to work?"

Reflective but vigorous, Margo took her hand. "I very much want to make love to you, but I had this flash – !"

"Can't we at least have some tea?"

"Put the kettle on – I'll set up again."

Kate stood in front of the stove, leaning over the rumbling kettle and shivering in a sudden fit of cold. She'd laid out the white cups on the table and hung the tea bags over the rims.

"Where's my girl?" Margo swept up behind her. Under her shirt, Kate's skin turned to sandstone at Margo's breezy touch. Margo hugged her from behind, her hand closing casually on Kate's breast. Kate pressed back against her, shivering.

"Are we really going right back to work?" Her ear tingled from Margo's warm breath, her nipple burned from her teasing fingers.

"The world should stop because you've finally made it with a woman?"

"Dead on its axis, ma'am."

Margo turned her around, kissed her lips. "You're charming, funny, sweet, and smart! You're perfect!"

"Kiss me again."

Completely happy, Kate felt Margo's tongue in her mouth, her soft and subtle lips.

"You kiss so humorously." Kate hugged her, laughing. "Your eyes change color all the time and one is smaller than the other. Did you know?"

Kate kissed Margo's eyes, sadness howling in her chest. She kissed Margo's forehead and cheeks, then slipped the lady's small, satiric smile into her mouth.

"You've the nicest mouth, Margo. I love your big hands."

Those wide, painty hands moved casually on Kate's shoulders and back. In their wake, pain came, flowing into Margo-made channels.

Margo poured water in the white cups. "Come on, now, have your tea."

Kate refused to sit. "I want to serve you."

"Sorry, darling, I've just poured the water."

Kate ran to Margo and ecstatically kissed her worn face. Margo kissed her dutifully back. "Drink up, will you?"

"I think we should celebrate!"

Margo pushed herself back from the table and balanced daringly on the hind legs of her chair.

"There is a bladder in the bottom left-hand corner of a painting by Margo Schwartz. A bladder in my painting. My reputation as one of the better contemporary artists is at stake, and you, in your light and girlish way, suggest we celebrate."

She pushed Kate cheerfully from the kitchen.

"But everything is different," Kate cried. "I don't want to do a zombie stint today!"

Margo switched on the lights. "Don't want, don't want, don't want," she teased. "You're a baby, my love." She unbuckled Kate's belt and the button of her fly. "A charming, delightful baby." She took off Kate's shirt.

"We'll have a late supper – go out, stay in, do anything you want."

Kate stepped onto the platform. "I have to go to my parents tonight."

"That's Elizabeth's line, sweetheart." Margo dipped the brush in the black paint. "Your line is, 'Let me go, let me go, Harry-husband will kill me if I'm not home by dark.'"

Kate whispered: "I really do have to go."

Margo strode up to the platform, leaned on a hard leg.

"You're the same age as Elizabeth, are you not? Well, then, you do not have to go to your parents' house. At the age of thirty-five, one is drawn to one's ancestral shit heap by desire, not duty."

Horrified by Margo's tone of vicious contempt, Kate concentrated on the bridge of her nose. "I feel I should go."

"Uptight, baby-bottle-sucking cunts – the two of you! Same half-assed guilty look as Elizabeth. Of course, she can't live without the weekly family dinner; can't live unless she can drag herself back here more dead than alive every seven days. And now you! Jesus! I'm down on my knees for my luck."

"I can come tomorrow morning, if you won't mind the baby."

Margo pulled her off the platform, roughly kissed her, then pushed her away.

"Oh, Margo," Kate cried. "You don't understand!"

"More than you think." She went to the couch and flung herself down. "Everything, in fact." She was asleep in a minute and snoring gently.

Kate dressed and then stood at the head of the couch, looking down at Margo's tired face, her big hands folded with casual reverence on her bare chest. Kate bent and kissed the battered thumb.

Margo opened one eye. "Never mind," she murmured; "you're a sweet, sweet child."

Valery rang her boots on crisp sidewalks beneath a starry night. Strode on jaunty lover's legs through the Oriental arch, through the brooding columns of municipal buildings.

At the head of the subway stairs she paused by a poster that told with Asian sky, helicopters, and two heads fused at the lip; the female bent, the male bending, of the glories of the hunt.

Valery kissed the female face. "Wake up, wake up," she cried; "it's better than you think."

Laughter flew out of her as she leaped the bottom five steps, lightly landing at the turnstile. Inserting the bright, gold coin in the slot, a sharp hip spinning the gate, she saluted the thundering train and parted the steel doors with a wave of her hand. Amen!

10

The judge's fist, slamming on the dining room table, terrified the candlelight and turned the wine in the tall, green bottles to howling oceans.

"Harry," the judge triumphantly cried, "you're a young man on the go."

Slowly, Mary Edwards lifted her head. Slowly, her dark eyes, hugely magnified behind her glasses, focused on her husband's red face. What was the matter with him? How dare he pound the table? Her eyes said this, not her lips, for she was miles underwater and nailed to a cement block. Her bony fingers crawled. Kate pushed the glass of shivering wine up to her fingertips.

"Ah, Kate," sang the Irish voice, your mother's near dead from the pain in her back."

Sara's soft, calamitous voice speeded the beat of Kate's heart.

"We were changing the sheets as we always do, the first thing after breakfast on Monday morning, when Mrs. Edwards let out a groan. I didn't know what the matter was, but I could see that the pain was terrible. I think she wrenched her back lifting a corner of the mattress, just tugging it up."

Now a week had passed and the pain was no better. "No better, hey, Ma?"

Kate drank her wine and asked Harry for a puff of

his cigar. She smiled at him through the silver branches of the candelabra. The candlelight glowed beautifully in the gold depths of the dining room table and in her mother's glasses when she pushed her brooding head forward and up. Saw Harry in the glasses, her father too. Both smoking cigars. Harry leaning toward the corner of the table and telling about his lunch with Dean Bender, her father leaning back. Behind them thin, threadbare golden curtains spread across the wide windows.

Between her father and mother in her old place, across from her husband, Kate felt all right tonight. She was no longer angry with her mother for drowning through time. Didn't care who'd early gotten to her and kicked the bright surface of her confidence to pieces. That event was over and what remained, remained.

It remained – the broken person whose fine blond hair sifted over the dim brow, a strand bending over the rim of the wineglass and floating on the red surface. There at the head of the rich table, the pieces carefully selected from long years of wreckage, was a living statue, but she, Kate, was here, and that very afternoon hadn't she traveled miles through dark tunnels, climbed hundreds of stairs and up the side of a big, beautiful woman? Her body had moved, felt, secreted moisture and the same sharp smells that had come off Margo. She had made Margo groan and groan.

Kate watched her mother's fingers rescue the bright strand of hair, squeeze out drops of wine, and fit it back between the rubber notches of the Woolworth's bobby pin. Years and years ago, still a girl, adoring her father, but having to leave, having to marry, the elegant, beautiful girl drowned herself and erected a statue to her memory. Her husband shoved it from place to place. Her young daughter played in front of it, climbing occasionally onto its lap to adjust the statue arms in an embrace. When the daughter grew older, she wept and wept for the drowning.

Kate smiled at her mother and took her hand. She waited tensely, fearing an ambush, for she was not on guard as usual, not all clenched and girded against the sadness that howled through her whenever the statue tried to move its arms, tried to ease with blurry words the guilt and shame that poured out of its eyes. *Your mother's nearly dead from the pain in her back.*

Sara had observed her from across the kitchen, taking in her handsome tweed jacket, her jeans and boots. "You've some nerve coming to your mother's table looking like a hippy bum," the housekeeper remarked.

"Two different things," Kate mumbled, unoffended."

Stomach in, shoulders back, Kate stood by the pantry door, swinging it out and back. She would like to lead this humble woman out of the dullness, but blind, scuttling, this person, female, grown old in domestic service, sleeping out the decades on a narrow box-spring bed in the smallest room in the house, this person would not renounce her Lord's wounds, would not look past or move beyond his violent stapling.

Her sister had entered a convent, but Sara, voyaging across the sea, wanted gold. Gold for her crippled mother, shoes and dark, wool coats for the nephews and nieces, for herself, a dark, musty tunnel for the future.

Drying her washed hands on the seat of her pants, Kate bowed respectfully to the old Irish housekeeper who'd brought her up, brought her down through pain, death, and the ugly, flapping noises of the wounded. She asked after her mother's cough, her stomach pains, for there was always something that kept her mother's eyes turned round in her head, as if her body were a conquered people, sullenly mutinous in one part or another, always.

A mistake, it knew, to have drowned the young girl. A tragedy to die such a long, long life.

Kate gripped the dry, thin hand in triumph. Pain was pain. It had happened. It was finished and she was alive to walk and talk.

Kate beamed at Harry through the silver candelabra. This evening when she'd met him on the corner – he was coming from the dean's club and she from Margo's – he'd looked so solid and adventurous with the bruise on his cheekbone. He'd grinned, seeing her, and stuck out his hand. They shook hands laughing, then ambled down the street, like comrades, like pranksters threading their way home.

Harry had remarked on the different styles of architecture, presented in miniature on the narrow house fronts. He pointed out a Florentine palace, a French chateau, and across the street, a pair of lions crouched before Roman gates, their heads grandly turned from the plain, red brick front of Kate's childhood home. The smallest house on the street, primly distinguished by its narrow windows and simple door.

They'd stood between the lions as Harry described the long lunch.

In a quiet, small dining room, hung with tapestries and lit by elegant chandeliers, Dean Bender had sat down at table with Harry as though with a toad. In his heart he hated Harry as the Trojan horse that had opened in the night. There had been such damage done to his buildings, windows smashed and furniture broken. A young professor's manuscript had been destroyed – there was a copy at home but still the malice was unspeakable – and, finally, there was Harry himself, the sponsor of the whole damned African American inclusion program, viciously turned on by his young champions and beaten.

Harry had silently stared at the hypocrite, who shaded his eyes with his hand, who averted his face, who practically choked every time he put food in his mouth.

The law school had been ruined. Politics had flooded the scholastic frame that the dean had laboriously constructed and he had no interest in floating with the wreckage.

Incredulous, hooting with cold laughter as he described the scene to Kate, Harry couldn't believe the arrogance that had fastened over the man like a suit of armor. It wasn't shame that kept the dean's face lowered and his head turned to the side. The fact that Harry was sitting among the French rugs and English chairs unable to piss – the fact that the dean was doing what he had promised he wouldn't do – was not the result of conscience but of fear.

Harry stood between the lions, each hand closed on a stone nose. The dean heated the tips of his asparagus with his downward raging eyes because he'd lost!

Kate leaned back on the lion's haunch, feeling the cold of the stone pass slowly through her jacket and jeans. Harry faced her, talking excitedly. Cars shot from behind his broad back, the roof of her house looked over his shoulders, and when he shifted, the window of her mother's bedroom showed itself, sweet with light.

The dean would do this, he would do that. Everything would be done that needed to be done if Harry would only use his influence sensibly.

There were to be no more outbreaks of senseless violence. No more publicity!

Harry elaborated with bitter humor. Dean Bender thought him an opportunist, a sleazy nobody from the sticks who was capable of using the newspapers to get his way. And yet it was Dean Bender in his snotty club, surrounded by his peers, in turn surrounded by their ancestors hung up on the ornate walls, who thought and operated like a gangster. The only thing that was stopping him from getting rid of Harry and every black student in the place was his terror that Harry would expose him to the newspapers.

"The indignation of being caught," note Harry, "puffed him up with all the intensity of a very moral man."

"Caught?" Kate looked up at him questioningly, her mind shying from the thought that, besides the wreckage and the rage, there'd been a death.

"But don't you see, Kate? Bender precipitated all the violence by *calling in* the police."

"Yes, I see that, but since he's was leaving in June, why would he care?" She pressed tensely back against the stone lion, not wanting to be told that the dean was a criminal.

Past Harry's shoulder, Kate saw her mother standing at her window. She'd just had her bath, Kate knew, and wore her black velvet hostess gown, the sleeves and hem trimmed with gold ribbon. She wore gold slippers and the perfume that winter, spring, summer, and fall scented her wake with roses.

He grinned cockily. "Well, honey, he doesn't want his friends to think him a fool."

Kate waved at the house. Her mother's gaze fell on them dimly, through miles and miles of bleak air. In the fall, when Harry was dean, a reporter might snap their pictures. Bright images in the news, but dim to the statue's eyes, drifting raggedly by.

"Come on, Mary," Judge Edwards cajoled, holding up his wineglass. "We're drinking to your extraordinary son-in-law."

Kate looked sharply at her father as he filled Harry's wineglass, saying that it would be disastrously naive for the young and able Gracchus to lose sight of the fact that, once launched as a liberal dean, he could not be too skillful a navigator, for both sides would try to shoot him out of the water, the African American student body as well as the senior faculty. He gazed down the table at his wife. "Darling, ring the bell."

Her mother's hand on the stem of the wineglass waiting for the toast to her extraordinary son-in-law shifted with incredible slowness to the bell.

Kate banged the bell and stood, taking her mother's plate. "You're so cynical, Dad!" As she reached for his plate, she looked away from his confident, frank face.

"You're too kind, Kate." He drank his wine with intense satisfaction. "I'm downright prejudiced! If I were in Harry's shoes, I'd kick every one of them on this new program out." He gripped Harry's shoulder. "This guy's been walking a tightrope for those students' sake, he's the one friend they've got, and they turn on him, five of them, and physically attack him. Even you can't condone that!"

"They were terrified, Dad!"

"Five of them!" The judge pounded the table. His emotion went beyond rhetoric.

The silver rattled on the plates as Kate caught Harry's aroused, pugnacious look. She remembered the violent way he'd slammed the grocery boy to the street.

Now he said: "I'll tell you one thing. I'll never get myself locked up in a room with them again."

"But you are so passionate about this," she half whispered. "You ought to understand." He stared at her from a vengeful distance.

"I was passionate and I got shat on."

"You're damned right, Harry! I'd find a way to get those bums if I were you. They ought to be shot!" Kate turned with the plates.

"They probably will be shot, eventually, Dad – by the police. Like James Eaton! Oh God, you're so unfair ... "

Underneath the Judge's gilded geniality was the tough face of a man who had years ago thrown his hook high and scrambled, hand over hand, to the remote ledge he now commanded. He snarled at his daughter.

"Oh, wake up, Kate!"

Suddenly Mrs. Edwards gasped and began to cough. Screwing up his eyes, the judge watched his wife as though there were an exact moment to come to her aid.

"I don't want to wake up to your world!" Kate cried.

"Then, get on the other side!" he said contemptuously, looking her over. "You're certainly dressed for it."

His eyes fixed on his wife, he rose in his chair. "But you can't very well be on one side with our young warrior on the other."

The pantry door shot open and stuck. Sara entered on a track of kitchen light, a glass of water in her hand.

"Drink," the judge cried, holding it to his wife's lips.

Mary Edwards was choking, her hands clutching her throat.

"But she hasn't eaten anything," Kate cried. "I've been watching." She looked desperately at Harry.

"She's choking on a crumb."

Judge Edwards pulled the chair out from the table, bent his wife over her knees, and pounded her back.

"It's out," Sara cried. "I saw it."

"Ah, Mary," the judge said tenderly, patting her back. He took off her glasses and wiped the lenses with his handkerchief.

Sara touched the bent back, then cleared away the steak platter. "You'll be all right now, Mrs. Edwards," she crooned as the door swung over behind her. Kate followed with the plates.

She returned to see Mary Edwards sitting sideways to the table, her arms folded, looking down at the floor.

"There it is," she cried vigorously. "On the edge of the rug – a bit of crust." She hauled round and smiled radiantly at Kate. "The pain in my back is gone! How queer!"

Kate wanted to huddle behind the candelabra and chat with her mother about her back. For the first time in ages, her mother was standing in a patch of sun and Kate

141

would have liked to idle there, smiling, but her father's mocking voice stung her cheek and spun her round. He sat confidently, his knee resting against the edge of the table.

"I was worried about you for a while, Harry. I thought, Christ, this guy's so earnest, so wet behind the ears, that he'll let himself be strapped to the mast and go down with the ship." He saluted nobly and put his hand over his heart. "But now I see that you're right in there pitching, boy! You're a nervy pirate!"

Harry emerged from the clouds of cigar smoke he'd exhaled round his head. The bitter distance of his gaze, his mean smile, surprised the judge. He raised his glass and stood: "A toast to us pirates!"

Harry sat down, leaned back.

The judge smiled coldly. "I wince for your ship."

"Sir?"

"The chair that you're just about to destroy by leaning back in that manner is a valuable antique, over two hundred years old, in fact."

Harry swept forward.

"Oh, sit back," Mary Edwards said, gaily waving. "Sit the way you want. It's my chair and I couldn't care less." Her hand patted his. "I knew you were a pirate the minute I saw you – do you remember I called you Roger?" She lifted her wineglass. "I'd rather toast a pirate than an extraordinary what have-you."

"You're a rich, Spanish galleon," her husband said derisively. "What do you know about it?"

"I find these two pirates delightful." She smiled graciously, turning her bright, big head from one to the other.

"Ah, you're drunk."

Mary Edwards grinned devilishly at Harry. "He's still got the manners he was born with."

The judge fumed. "What's gotten into you, for God's sake?"

"That dreadful pain has gone from my back. You must have whacked something straight – I feel marvelous."

Sara poked her head through the door. "Will you be having your coffee here or in the library, Mrs. Edwards?"

Kate stood at the back of her mother's chair.

"We'll take our coffee in the library so that you can get at the table, Sara." A low, sunny voice full of warmth – a sun remembered from certain parts of Kate's childhood, although it had come out rarely and mourned while it shone.

Dreamily, she was recalling how, long in the past, one swung on the doorknob, tumbled into the hall, and yelled, "Mother?" up the dim stairs. Pulling up and around the long, mild curve of banister, the sound rang excitedly in one's ears. And then one came into the dim room where Mary Edwards sat through the afternoon at the end of the couch.

"Hello," she'd murmur, looking up from her book. "How are you?" You are happy, said her gloomy smile, but I am miserable. And there one stood at the edge of a black hole floundering under the sudden weight of one's excitement. True, the sun is marching through the streets in triumph. A man blew a ram's horn in the park. And, Mother, as a girl you ran like the wind.

Never mind, said the bowed head, said the large glasses. Her mother mourned with her book and her

143

glasses. But for whom? Not for the blowers of horns, oh, no! Crass and arrogant, they walked their glittering faces right by, saying, get a grip on yourself, get out of the corner, get out here where life can get at you. What on earth is so bad about life?

Then, by the waters of Babylon, the tall orange lamp was lit behind the couch and Sara brought up tea and cinnamon toast. To cheer them up, said her mother, to cheer them up on this cold, gray, miserable afternoon. The arm and back of the leather couch tolerantly enclosed the gloomy lady, its worn, wrinkled skin agreeing that life was no gag. Sad, sad, sad, said the horn-rimmed pools where the lady's eyes drowned.

Her tongue coated with butter and cinnamon, young Kate let her troubles sprinkle the surface of her mother's pain and listened to the beautiful voice rise and fall as though in a dream.

Now, once again in the library, Kate bent and smelled the leather arm of the chair in which she sat, her booted legs sprawled in front of her. She watched her father pour out brandy and felt with light, little swoops of her hands the satiny leather sides of the chair. Margo's soft hide pulled to satin. Kate licked the leather, then dried the arm with her sleeve. Margo's taste was so delicious, in her mouth, in her –

Her mother's face jutted past the orange lamp. "What's the matter, Kate?" Her gold foot jumped out from her gown.

Kate took coffee from Sara, looked vaguely at her mother across the broad silver tray. "What?"

"Are you sick?" asked Mrs. Edwards.

"Of course not."

"But you groaned."

"Sorry."

Her father put down the brandy on the desk beside her and took in, with a humorous shake of his head, her stretched-out legs and her hands shoved into the pockets of her jeans.

"My darling Katey, what a sight you'll be among the teapots." He tweaked her nose and sat down on the couch beside his wife. "A very sullen dean's wife among the teapots." Liquor and food had warmed his mockery. He loved combat and so did she, no longer fearing, as she had when a child, his hard, hard anger.

He crossed his legs, let his head tip back, nearly touching the frame of a landscape she'd painted one summer at art school, which had won her a prize as the session's most improved painter. Judge Edwards loved northern Connecticut, could see the glaciered countryside beneath the severe greens, grays, and yellows. Could see, when she brought the painting home, her future. He hung it right up and marveled, brandy riding his chest, at the fame and fortune that, if he were any judge of art (he was not), would inevitably be hers if she simply worked. Work, work, work! How could she miss?

Time after time she'd sabotaged his zinging projections of her success, but she'd go along too. A young girl on the third floor, she'd shared a bathroom with Sara and worked coldly for grades, hour after hour, coming down to the library before bed to have a few sips of brandy and a vision implanted in her tight, high-speed brain. She would be: the top woman surgeon, historian, painter, physicist, lawyer, mathematician – pick one, sang her father, and with work, endless, grinding work, the world would be her oyster.

When she'd worked on Wall Street in a bright office that overlooked the harbor, she heard twice a day the cart that the messenger dragged come creaking down the corridor and knew that he would say, "More straw," for he was a writer and told her that she was the miller's daughter thrust among the straw to spin it into gold. She couldn't read fast enough to make space for more documents on her desk, table, or the broad sill of her spectacular window, so he'd stack the new material on the floor, very slowly and carefully, and was sorry that he wasn't the cranky dwarf that would save her ass. He brought in Coke and hero sandwiches and gave her puffs of grass in the supply room to get her through.

One afternoon she went off to the messenger's wedding. She ate Greek food, smashed glasses, and telephoned her father to tell him that she'd thought of an epitaph for her gravestone: "The world was her oyster," she brayed through the mouthpiece.

She glared at him. "You ought to take that awful painting down."

He softly belched. "I should think that the evidence of such talent would inspire you to get back to some sort of work."

Kate took the silver letter opener off the desk, held it by the point, and flicking her hand, threatened to play mumblety-peg with the evidence of her talent.

Harry turned from the desk, where he'd been reading with his back to the room, and took the letter opener from

Kate's hand. He sat on the arm of her chair and went back to the paper.

The judge observed her calmly. "Do you know that when you picked up that letter opener you looked like a common criminal?"

"Did I?" she brightly replied. "How interesting."

"Were you at some sort of demonstration today, or what?"

Her hand brushed the back of Harry's leg and stayed against the warm flannel. "I was down in Chinatown as usual, getting my portrait painted."

Scotch, wine, and now brandy had launched Mrs. Edwards to a blurred and pleasant place. "Darling, how marvelous. I want to see it."

The judge leaned out from the chair, his face sharp after fact. Would he know the name of the artist who was painting her? Kate supplied the name, inwardly ridiculing her sudden panic.

Her father studied the books above her head. Criminals, reading their fate from his face, might think that he heroically bombarded justice with his mind, that his strong conscience might burn through sleep in a spasm of reconsideration. And Harry repeatedly said that her father, although appointed by a god-awful hack, was clear, fair, and essential in his decisions.

But Kate's mind contracted in the assault of his will and became a sullen surface, thick as a turtle's shell.

"I've heard of Margo Schwartz," her father said. He went to the bookcase behind Kate. "I saw her work last year, I think." His fingers tapped on the book backs behind Kate's head. "Here's the catalog."

Kate advised herself to run, but Harry, still sitting on one arm of her chair, and her father, now perching on the other, seemed grim guards at her gates.

"My god, how ugly!" The judge passed the catalog to Harry, who looked interminably. Kate's hand shot out and snatched the book.

There was Elizabeth sitting at a desk, her large elbow and hand supporting her head, which looked out at the artist, the eyes peeking through her bangs like a Crazy Jane.

The judge bent over Kate's back. His hot breath, smelling strongly of cheese and brandy, made her silently gag.

"Technically, that gal knows her stuff, but the way the light hits the eyes makes the expression so brutal."

Harry leaned, "That's a panicked look, I think."

"Oh, Harry, let me see," cried Mrs. Edwards, stretching out her arms. Taking the catalog, she looked a long time, her legs rustling in the lining of her skirt. "I know this face," she said, looking up. "It's Elizabeth Graves. How sad!"

The judge stretched out beside his wife. "How could you possibly tell who that is?"

Mary Edwards looked across at Kate. "What's happened to Elizabeth? She looks so sad."

"Crazy, you mean," sneered the judge.

"What's the difference?" Kate shouted, worried about Margo's use of light. Was she a simpleminded crank?

Harry touched her shoulder.

"Didn't you say that Margo has you looking into the light?"

Was he a traitor? Angrily, Kate turned on Harry, but saw a slow brandy consciousness in his pleasant eyes. "And you're getting yourself a winter tan with no strap marks."

"Shut up," she whispered, punching his arm.

Judge Edwards stood and regarded his daughter solemnly.

"A few questions, please."

Yes, a portrait of his daughter was being executed without clothes under hot, bright lights.

Yes, the painting would be shown at the museum's annual exhibit of contemporary artists.

Incredulous, hollow in the cheek, the judge turned to his wife. He'd just seen their daughter step from the rim of all profitable experience, watched her go to pieces in the slums, where living was sheer slobbery, unmeasured by any rule that mattered.

I have left off weaving at the loom for greater things, do you praise me?

The judge brushed lint off his trousers, then his shoes, finally his hands. "It's beyond my comprehension why anyone would want to have themselves painted as ugly."

"Beyond mine too," Kate said stoutly.

He smiled coldly. "Apparently not."

So stout and calm, yet Kate's interior was filling with tears, both handles of the waterworks department were full throttle. Dumb broad gonna cry – peel off the armor before she drowns.

But her apparent calm had infuriated her father.

"What's the point?" he suddenly shouted. "Exposing yourself – it's horrid and aggressive – a girl of your

149

background!" He took a step toward her and stopped as she raised one booted leg. "What the hell is it supposed to prove beyond the fact that you're a ... a what? A cancer casualty?"

"I represent an idea, you fool! Not just myself."

"Every last, ever-loving detail of you blown up to billboard size? What idea can transcend that?"

"Ideas don't hang over things like God. They're in the expression, in the buttons on the shirt." Kate drew up both her legs as her father loomed over her.

"The buttons on what shirt?" His breathing was shrill. "You've had a bad time, a very bad time, but why should all the world know it?'"

Reins of will kept her head up and her eyes, however madly blinking, on his. "Women have had a bad time, an extremely bad time, and all the world should know it."

"Maimed Womanhood," he sneered. "The title of the painting will be 'Maimed Womanhood,' and under that, I suppose, they'll put your name and the date. Tell me, have you officially joined the women's movement?"

Behind her legs, Kate felt bruised and sick and ugly. "Not officially."

"But you intend to."

"I'm a woman, Dad, I was joined up at birth."

His hands cut the air in a sharp, furious gesture, spinning Kate's brandy glass from the table. Kate watched the amber liquid flowing into the rug.

"Ah, Christ." He picked up the glass and threw it into the fireplace.

"Hey," Mary Edwards mumbled from the corner, of the couch. "Hey, get a towel."

150

The judge was on his way, but paused at the door, pointing grimly at Harry. "That's all your reluctant allies need, you know. You won't be dean with 'Maimed Womanhood' hanging for all the world to see. Not in a pig's eye, you won't."

Harry put his arm around Kate. "Fuck the teapots," he growled.

Kate was suddenly in pain. Wet under her arms, between her legs, treading water with bursting lungs – but she hadn't cried – gas pains crimping her, freezing her ... don't worry, folks, the young woman may exit on her knees, but she'll be back.

Harry's hand slid down her head and back as she got up. "Excuse me," she gasped, running from the room.

11

At the foot of the stairs, bolts of gas doubled her over and she dropped to her knees. Gradually she straightened up, her shadow looming suddenly on the stairwell like a huge, sick, antique beast. Her father hurried by with paper towels and a pan of water. She ignored him and pulled her shoulders back and stood erect. Now she was a hunter with a stomach shrunk to the size of a pea. As the gas died in her gut, Kate made up her mind to call Margo.

She quickly climbed the stairs, stepped briskly across the hall, into her mother's room and between the twin beds, where she glanced at herself in the maple mirror that hung above the bureau a few feet off.

She sat on one bed, her feet resting on the siding of the other. The receiver was cold in her hand but her face in the mirror looked heroically disdainful of pain. She dialed information for the number of Margo Schwartz. Children, she thought, as the operator breathed lightly into the phone, are born to themselves as heroes. It is given them. But, growing older, the child must wander in strange lands where no one sees his crown.

There was no listing for Margo Schwartz residing anywhere in Chinatown. Kate hung up, then dialed another operator for the number of Elizabeth Graves. Her finger wrote the telephone number of Elizabeth across the maple headboard and dialed

As the days had passed in the hospital, Kate had rejoiced in her wound. The gods, she reasoned, flatten those they favor and the great were finally known by their suffering. Don't you see me? Don't you know me? By the newsstand in the subway, or in the park some dazzling day, one opens one's knapsack and whips out a crown.

Daa, daa! Oh, how the people stopped and rocked. They wept with joy and cried: "The queen lives!"

The phone rang and rang. Kate stared into the mirror – such a tough, confident face, what matter if Elizabeth answered and she must hang up? What matter if Margo was cold? A fall, not a death.

A quiet, mean voice said: "Yes."

"Margo?" A squeak, not a voice. Awful, awful to have called.

Who was this please? Oh, Kate. And where was she? Still at Mumsy and Dadsy's? Sweet. And how were Mumsy and Dadsy? And was Harry husband there? And how was he? Had Mumsy served up a good din-din? Were the servants behaving themselves? Mumsy's back? How terribly, terribly sad. Well, it was lovely of Kate to leave the swell family party and call her old friend Margo, but she really must go back or Mumsy and Dadsy will think her rude and that would be too terrible for words, now, wouldn't it?

"Why are you doing this?" Kate shouted as her mother came through the bedroom door and stood reproachfully between the tall, maple bedposts.

"My back," she murmured.

"I've got to go," Kate said.

"And why do you have to go?"

"My mother is here."

"Surely you're too old to scamper off the phone simply because your parent has walked into the room?"

Kate began to sweat. "She needs a heating pad – I really must hang up."

Ah, but why not let Margo have a few words with her mother? She knew an excellent back man and would like to pass along his name. Spirals of bad laughter filled Kate's ear. She hung up fast. Shit, the woman was crazy.

In the low-ceilinged white room, her mother's black gown and yellow hair were poster blatant. She carried a Scotch, almost black and brimming to the top of a large glass. Blocking the passage between the two beds, she regarded Kate mournfully.

"Your back?" Kate asked.

Mrs. Edwards looked directly at Kate for a long, long while. "The pain never goes away," she finally said as Kate's eyes dropped guiltily.

Over the beds or under, ignoble or no, any escape. Mrs. Edwards swayed against the bridge of Kate's legs, then sat down on the bed beside her. She took a long drink, then offered the glass. Still swallowing, her arm dropped over Kate's shoulders.

A tiny despairing sound happened in Kate's chest. As the liquor went down her throat, Kate felt herself dropping miles in cold, black air. She put the glass on the table and swung back over the bed. Kicking shut the bathroom door, she fell on her knees before the toilet and vomited, the bright leaping water soaking her face.

154

Mary Edwards opened the bathroom door and stood behind Kate like a zombie while Kate brushed her teeth, stood so close that Kate couldn't bend and spit into the sink without touching her. Scared to death, Kate pressed against the basin and gagged violently.

But what was she scared of? Pull up, damn you, up and out!

Kate inched out and wiped her mouth on a towel. "The last time you strained your back you used the heating pad. Don't you remember how it helped?"

Her mother brightened and pointed to the bathroom closet. "It's on the top shelf. It's pink."

"Get your nightgown on." Kate snapped on the closet light. "Get into bed – I'll get you all fixed up in a minute."

Kate idled in the closet. The smell of drugs was comforting and her mother had turned at her words and gone off docilely. The heating pad had a pink-and-white-striped flannel cover, like Cam's nightgown. Kate cheerfully slapped the pad against her leg, exploding dust as she came into the bedroom.

But her mother had lodged herself in the corner by the bureau, her face against the wall. Plug in the pad, turn down the bed, take down her mother's nightgown from the back of the closet door. Purposeful, yes, very, but dumb when she came up behind the stashed body with the drifting arms.

Desperately she wished not to touch! Do get that robe off please, before she shifts and comes crashing down.

Kate flicked back the bright hair and pulled the zipper down. The smell of roses sprang up between the treads, in the gap of gray skin, her mother's spine raked down. Kate hung the black nightgown round the docile neck, then lifted the big hands through the armholes. Now the portage.

"Walk backward," she whispered to her groaning mother. She'd taken hold of her waist and pulled her out from the corner – Kate was a big, strong girl with lots of tennis in her past, but Mary Edwards' sleeping hulk rolled back against her like a boulder, crashing them both into the bedpost. The pain, and her mother's inertness, infuriated Kate. With one last effort she swept her mother onto the bed, her trunk first and then her legs.

"Stupid old drunk," she gasped, then slipped the heating pad beneath the harsh spine. She drew the nightgown down the long, thin legs and pulled up the sheet. Glasses off, then velvet headband. Smoothing the bright hair, Kate discovered its softness, soft as Cam's.

Kate sat down on the opposite bed and studied the body spread out before her. She watched the fine brow and nose and touched the lovely hands. What had happened to her? Why was she so knocked down? The facts Kate knew were so few and common. Her mother's father treated her romantically, wept on her bed the night she was married, soon after took a mistress. But Mary Edwards had never taken a husband or been a mother to her child. Kate studied the queenly face. Women are marching in the streets, Ma, the sun blazes.

Kate picked up the phone again and dialed the number of Margo's loft. Absorbed, very mean.

"Yes."

"Homosexuality is an adolescent death box," Kate announced. "All the power you have over me is derived from my past. You're just an idea."

Margo mildly laughed. "Where are you, anyway? Still at Mumsy and Dadsy's? How cozy."

"Did you love your mother?" blurted Kate.

At the appropriate time Margo supposed that she had, but she must get off the phone, for Elizabeth had just put her key in the lock – oh, for that key in her lock. Ta ta!

Her mother, up on one elbow, was looking at Kate curiously. "Do you remember Keith Keere, darling?"

Kate vividly remembered that handsome blond man, an Australian officer, who sat with her mother, night after night, the year her father was in the Pacific, training fliers.

"He used to carry me up to bed."

"He adored you," her mother said dreamily.

For ages, it seemed, he would sit on the edge of Kate's bed and tell her stories about his life in Australia; his sheep farm where his many children worked and played and didn't give a rap about school. Kate was his little city chicken and after the war she must come and spend the summers with him. He tickled her, kissed her, and told her she was beautiful. He was Apollo, coating her with light.

Her mother tapped her hand. "You were miserable when he left. Do you remember how you cried?"

Kate pointed. "You cried!" God, how her mother had cried, in great bursts around the house. She'd weep and drink and drink and weep and go to bed without supper. Certainly Kate remembered the year of Apollo, after which Kate found her father cold and hated his edgy touch.

"Harry reminds me of Keith Keere," her mother said. "He adores you."

"I never should have married him." Kate took the

157

pillow from her father's bed and slipped it behind her mother's shoulders.

Mrs. Edwards hoisted herself and reached for her glasses. "You're a good nurse."

"I had a good teacher."

"Who?"

"You, of course, when I was in the hospital."

Mrs. Edwards looked pensively at Kate. "You were so brave. I was so impressed with you."

"You came every day for a month." Her mother pressed her hand.

"So I did."

"We almost finished *Anna Karenina*."

The operation had been performed in February. The sky was intensely blue in the frame of the window opposite her bed. The sharp, high sound of the wind, the boats on the river, and the traffic on the drive below evoked a huge and violent world behind her mother's low, warm voice.

Seen in the window behind her mother's head was a reckless smokestack, half a mile high in the cold sky.

"Burning more bodies," said the smart-ass resident one morning with a glance at the huge puffs of smoke. That the white smoke was transmuted bone, liver, sinus, that clogged and tortured cells were exploded in hot ovens and spiraled gaily through the atmosphere, was an appealing idea to Kate, although she did not express it to the odious little prick with mis-matched socks.

Her mother had come every afternoon at two, bringing the smell of the cold on her fur coat and books, pads, paints, pastries.

In mild pain, Kate loved the hospital routine. She

hadn't been brave because she didn't really hurt and because when she walked out of the hospital it would be the future and there she was a hero. In the future she was tried and chosen. She would live in a loft near the candy factories with the smell of cherry Life Savers coming under the heavy windows. In a bright, white space she'd turn her hand to writing and take care of Cam. Because even then, she knew.

When the nurse came in with her sleeping pill – cheerful eyes and a gold front tooth – no, she could not slip in another back rub, greedy thing – Kate knew she'd be leaving Harry.

When the nurse had remade the bed, spreading, through her exertions, the scent of lilacs throughout the room, Kate in her bandages and mild pain, in her safe room, thought radiantly of the trial that awaited her, that would take her from the edge of history, where she'd sullenly slouched, to its glorious center.

Mrs. Edwards sipped from the glass and passed it to Kate. "*Anna Karenina* almost finished me, poor woman."

"Tolstoy must have been a terrible moralist to have that full, firm, white neck that he loved severed by steel wheels." Kate passed back the glass. "All because she left her robot husband. It's outrageous, really."

Mrs. Edwards gazed moodily at her daughter. "One has to pay the piper, I suppose."

"So they tell us."

"Who, darling?"

"The masters, Ma! You know," she said, smiling ironically, "the men who organize everything, who write down the laws and build the gallows and hoist the ropes.

The guys who write the chilling moral tales. George Eliot would never thrust her heroine under a train."

Mary Edwards looked irritably at her hand. "That was inevitable, absolutely inevitable."

"Tolstoy certainly thought so, but I don't."

"Perhaps you will someday," her mother taunted. "After all, he was a genius."

Kate's face grew hot, then freezing cold. "He was a fool!"

Kate could feel her mother's rage un-crouched in her, coming up from the back of her cramped life like a wounded lioness.

"So are you a fool," she snarled.

"I am," Kate cried, "I admit it."

"Good! You should."

So irritable and haughty! Men had thronged round her once-beautiful body, her once-lovely face. The queen who had taken a dozen lovers and had once been heard to say – drunk, of course, her large black dog panting into her face, his paws trembling on her shoulders – "Even the dog wants to fuck me."

The dog, a dozen lovers, Christ, the queen itched and trickled with shameful need. Need needs. In truth, the pain of statue stillness is immense. Thousands of gallons of the best Scotch and non-stop vaginal traffic only begin to take off the edge. How do you realize the pain of a lifelong stall?

Kate looked grimly at her boots. "I never should have married Harry."

"Oh, God, Kate," Mary Edwards irritably cried. "You should be grateful."

"That's so terrible, Mother! That's a terrible attitude!"

Her mother seemed sick of Kate's emotion. "People aren't so much," she said wearily. "Hang on to him."

Mary Edwards turned on her side and drew her legs up, her face gone quite gray. For a few moments she seemed to shrink and when she wound out again, her eyes were horrified. She struggled free of the covers and pitched toward the bedroom door.

"What is it?" Kate watched the large hand pluck at the doorknob.

"Want David. Oh, God!"

Kate turned her mother around. "Go back to bed."

Mary Edwards flared silently.

"Please tell me what I can do for you."

"I want David!"

Slowly, resentfully, Kate went down the stairs. The alacrity of her father's response struck her as absurd. He bounded out of his chair, knocking her shoulder as he went through the door.

Harry stretched in his chair. "What's the matter, honey?" Kate took a sip of his brandy and picked up the novel her mother had been reading, threw it on the couch.

"Is your mother sick?"

"She thinks so."

"The old man sure stirred his stumps."

She eyed him viciously. "Sure did."

The judge came to the door and motioned gloomily to Harry. "I need your help."

Kate followed the men out into the hall and stopped with a weak cry.

Mary Edwards lay on her back at the foot of the stairs,

clutching her glasses. Her thin nightgown was hitched round her waist. Her father stopped and with a quick, gentle gesture pulled down the gown.

"She's dead!" Kate murmured.

Her father squeezed her hand. "Your mother's drunk, darling. But how the hell did she manage this? She wasn't so bad when she went to bed."

Harry took the legs as his father-in-law directed and moved carefully up the stairs. Judge Edwards hauled away, cursing his insensate wife. Pills, booze, all too much.

The two men collapsed when they'd gotten Mary Edwards under the covers. They sat side by side on the opposite bed, the judge panting violently. "That's a dead weight for you – incredible, hey?" He passed his handkerchief to Harry.

Kate stood between the bedposts holding her mother's glasses. "I thought she was dead."

"Dead drunk," her father grumbled, passing by. Harry followed him, then Kate sat down abruptly on the landing and began to cry.

Her father beckoned back to her sweetly from the library door.

"Katey, darling, you've seen your mother like this before." He came up the stairs and squeezed down beside her. "She's a tough old bird, you know, tough as they come."

Harry reached through the banister and took her hand.

"Why does she drink so much?" Kate gasped.

"She's always drunk too much, it's her way."

But her mother was so unhappy, Kate sobbed. Why did she have to be so unhappy?

Judge Edwards took her by the neck and shook her gently. "Your mother doesn't think of herself as unhappy." He looked at his son-in-law with humorous affection.

"You'll be carrying Kate to bed before long. All the women in this family are morose. Can't tell you why." He shrugged philosophically.

"So they're morose, so what?" mumbled Kate. "Carry them up to bed when they've had too much. We've got the strength to do it."

He stood and clicked his heels decisively. "Kate, my darling, knock it off. Your mother is having herself a good sleep. Now, come have some brandy."

A few minutes later Kate swung on the iron gate before the darkened house, hooting mournfully through her hands. Harry walked down the center of the street toward the avenue looking for a cab. A car turned into the street and sped down on him, its bright headlights sculpting horns from his thick, tousled hair.

"Coo COO," Kate hooted, swinging back and forth. Her eyes traveled up the long side of the opposite apartment house into the canyon of brilliant night sky. Bright clouds flew past in joyous migration. Nature was fast: rivers, wind, the blood in her arteries. Nature delighted in transition, its glorious game.

But, the house behind her, both parents asleep on one of its floors, resisted the play, the bricks diminishing with a rancorous, dry rasp, year by year.

A flash of yellow as the cab drew down. Harry pushed

open the cab door and waved to her. The gate swung out, Kate jumped, folded herself, slid in.

She looked back across the pavement to the dark house and hooted softly. Harry took her hand. "Hey, owl! It's not the last time."

"It's always the last time," she said thoughtfully. "Always."

12

The floor of the kitchen pitched wildly under Kate's feet. She was startled but noticed that the stove, the fridge, and the kitchen counters all seemed to be holding their own. She hung onto the door and encouraged Harry in his struggle with the ice trays.

Harry lumbered uphill to the sink, rolled back against the table, turned, and tried the passage backward. Got the water going.

"But, of course, the driver was a girl." Kate went back to their argument begun behind the plastic partition of the speeding taxicab. Glossy black curls, a calm, steady foot on the accelerator, and spied through the scratched plastic, definitely a pair of feminine eyes.

The ice cracked in the trays. Harry turned off the water, managed two glasses from the dishwasher, and filled them with cubes.

"Pitch-black in the cab," he murmured. "Couldn't see eyes."

"I could clearly see when the streetlight shone in. I saw feminine eyes and brows."

Harry poured out Scotch, then whizzed a kitchen chair under his huge, rubbery weight.

"You saw the eyes," he crooned, "but didn't see the

165

thick, hairy hand grabbing bills in the slot. Fingers like carrots, for Christ's sake."

It was a girl driving, Kate insisted. A real pirate who threaded her way through the traffic like a pro. She glared at him. A real pirate, not bogus and talky like herself. You wouldn't find her jumping down marriage holes and getting drunk in her parents' house. That kind of girl was pushing through saloon doors at the end of an honest day's work, right through a roomful of hostile men to the bar. That kind of girl had a gin or Scotch before she went home to take care of the kid or study law or some other tremendously admirable thing.

Tears of admiration for the girl and loathing for herself blurred Kate's vision.

Harry smiled at her fondly.

"Come sit on my lap."

"No!"

"All right, the driver was a girl. Now, come here." Kate jumped off the counter and hugged him fiercely. "Do you really love me?"

"More and more,"

"Do you think I'm sexy?"

He kissed her neck and eyes. "Terribly sexy."

Kate remembered his hair lit up by the car lights and she molded his curls into two points. "There, I've given you horns."

She sobbed at his kind, inquiring look and hid her head on his shoulder.

"You're exhausted, honey! I'm putting you to bed."

Kate clung to his neck as he toted her. Yawning, gently cursing, he made his way through the dark apartment

166

and for once, feeling his strength and grace, she did not resent his natural advantages, the aristocracy inherent in his favored genes. It was an uphill trudge of the will to hate the strength that held one up, but in the letdown, clinging to his neck like a monkey on the mast, guilt and wretchedness shot through her.

The overhead light swept over the ceiling, and Kate, sitting cross-legged on the broad bed, hid her face in her arms. Harry shut the bedroom door and softly slipped the bolt. Standing over her, he took off his jacket and tie.

"You're not planning to sleep in your boots?"

She peered up at him. "It's the truth that I've given you horns."

His Rose Bowl mitt went up to his hair. His conscientious expression made her die.

"They're still on the small side," she mocked, "because I've just started them today."

"You were posing for Margo today."

"I didn't pose one minute."

Harry sat down on the bed and looked at her curiously. "What did you do?"

She bent her burning face over her knees. "I told you. I spent the afternoon growing you horns."

"Horns, horns, horns," mused his soft, southern voice, "why does the lady keep talking about horns?"

He slapped his leg. "Adultery! Holy Christ! You're telling me you've committed adultery!"

He charged into the bathroom, slamming the door behind him. Kate heard the shower and, moments later, the doorknob turning frantically. She drew a pillow in front of her as Harry flew out, wet and gleaming under the ceiling light. He stood before her, lashing a towel around his waist.

"Didn't you tell me that you spent the afternoon with Margo?"

She nodded.

"You've been seeing guys down there? A guy? Tell me."

Two women on a red rug. How could she tell him?

"Tell me!" She let herself go limp between his hands.

"Margo," she whispered into the roar of his breathing. "I've been with her."

The blue towel slipped down his leg. He caught it, held it vaguely, then sat and stared at her wonderingly.

Kate burst into tears. "I've ruined our marriage," she sobbed.

He took her hand and held it absently. "No, you haven't. What are you talking about?"

Dripping off her chin, her tears made a pattern on the bedspread. "I've betrayed you."

Harry shrugged and continued to hold her hand.

"What's the matter with you?" Kate challenged.

"I'm thinking."

She jumped up, suddenly furious. "What do you mean, you're thinking? What the fuck good can that do?" She paced up and down the room, then climbed up on the bed behind him. "I've betrayed you and ruined our marriage," she passionately cried. "What are you going to do about it?"

He turned to her quietly. "Shut up for a minute, will you?"

She threw herself back on the bed. "I've committed

adultery," she moaned through her hands. "I'm a lesbian and he doesn't even care ... "

"Does one trip to France make you a Frenchman?"

She stared at him, horrified. "You're so cynical!"

"Me!"

"You don't give a shit that our marriage is over."

"Our marriage isn't over, you nut."

She pressed her cheeks in agony. "But I've been with another person and I liked it."

She clutched at his hand in distress. "The minute I saw her at the funeral, sitting on the couch with the lampshade tipped up, I got this intense feeling, here!" She put her hand on her lower stomach. "The next day I went out, bought these clothes, these boots, and I went downtown when I knew Elizabeth wasn't going to be there. I talked Margo into making love because I thought it was a political act, like an initiation rite or a sacred oath that would bind us like sisters. But ha, ha! It was sexual and I loved it. It was like doors opening." She looked at him with guilty defiance. "I loved it, Harry, and I want to do it again."

Kate whipped under the spread, drawing it tight over her head. "I'm going to get a drink." He patted her ass. "Want one?"

"Yes," she moaned, "and Triscuits."

When he'd gone, she tossed back the covers and looked desolately at the bright ceiling light. Springing at the switch, she flicked it off, then lit the room from the bathroom by half opening the door. She drew the curtain across the window and was back under the spread when Harry came through the door, glasses clinking cheerfully on the tray. He'd spread cream cheese on the Triscuits and mixed the Scotch with soda in just the way she liked.

She struggled against tears and yelled that Harry wasn't normal, wasn't a real man. A real man would stand between his wife and promiscuity like a dog before a bone.

Harry lit a cigar and swung into bed beside her, stuffing pillows behind his back.

"Listen, if Margo were a man, you'd have thrown me out the window by now."

He sighed, sipping his drink.

"Why aren't you reacting?"

"I don't know how to react."

"You don't consider Margo a threat because she's a woman. We're just two freaks to you."

"That's not true," he staunchly cried.

"When you thought Margo was a man, you were exploding all over the place."

He looked at her nervously. "Did Margo make a pass at you?"

Kate blushed and turned her head away. "Are you sure you really want to hear? It's almost dawn, maybe we should go to sleep and talk tomorrow."

He took her hand. "Mrs. Quinn will get up with Cam and take her to the park." He glanced at the brightening window. "It would be nice to talk and talk ..."

It was lovely to drink as the soft, smoky air of the room grew lighter. As Kate relaxed beside Harry, she was aware of the softly flaring curtain and her husband's patient breathing. She held her head for a moment, tapped it, and said with a wry smile:

"Of course, it all began up here. It began when I

thought of Valery St. John my first year at college. I took a short story course and this was the very first thing I wrote – do you really want to hear? It was something like: 'My feet are bloody. I have walked barefoot this past week (it is in the middle of March) and today I climbed Robard's Hill. Tonight I shall sleep in my clothes with my shield at my side and dream that in Cuchulain's battle car, side by side, we smite the enemy low.'"

"We? Who was with Valery?"

"I didn't know when that spun out. It turned out to be a young chick called Cynthia Chubb, a Boston girl with milkweed hair and pale, watery eyes. She roomed next door to Valery, adored her in glimpses and glances for months, and gradually inserted her trepidating self into Valery's life.

"Valery was an arrested tomboy who loved physical adventure and whiskey. She read two books: *Tom Sawyer* and *The Odyssey* – only when drunk – aloud, over and over again. She despised women and therefore her future, so at the end of the story – the story turned into a novel – she got terribly drunk and ran her car off a mountainous country road. Cynthia was left with her two books and her ashes, which she let fly from Robard's Hill."

Kate laughed nostalgically. "I loved those two characters. I worked for a long time trying to get the thing in shape to publish. But as it was the idea of Valery I was interested in and not so much being a writer, I finally stowed the book and went to law school."

The curtain flew up as a sharp, light rapping sound went across the window. "It's raining," Kate cried delightedly.

"What did Valery look like?"

171

"She looked like a warrior, of an ancient tribe, fierce and tall, naturally."

Harry stroked her shoulder. "Wouldn't the lesbian feminists have loved Valery!"

"And, brother, her soul would sure have been soothed by them. But there weren't women like that in her time and so she had to die. She died in me until recently. She was sleeping soundly until the hospital. Maybe it was the strong drugs and the physical shock to my system. At any rate, Valery just stood up in my guts after all these years and started to howl. Action, she wants, and fucking and the speedy glorification of the female race."

The memory of waking from the great frost that had statued her filled her with violent joy. "It's deep, you know, and it's been on tracks from a long way back, long before I met you, so you see, it isn't a betrayal of you, it's a finding of me."

"Are you in love with Margo?"

"Looking at Margo, feeling her, thinking about her, I feel more myself. I feel great. And I think that's because she reflects what I could become. Because there's something to be, right now, that hasn't been before, and Margo's on that track. So is Elizabeth."

Harry looked at her doubtfully.

"Lesbianism as a political act," Kate murmured. "Margo laughed at me, but the idea of women really digging each other, intellectually, emotionally, physically, is a terribly exciting thing and it's never been! I can't think of any parallel to David and Jonathan in the Bible. Literature is filled with female martyrs but can you think of a famous female friendship?"

"Not right offhand."

"That's what's so exciting about Margo and Elizabeth. I know they bitch at each other, but they are not a defensive thing, shoulders to weep on and all, they're comrades in arms against the world!" She clapped her hands.

"Oh, Harry, I'm in love with them!"

Harry smiled nervously. "I can understand that."

"It's obvious, isn't it? Homosexuality isn't meaningful to you because the whole show is a mirror for men and always has been."

"An unfavorable mirror for most men." He clicked his glass against hers. "We have all been screwed by the white warrior male, my dear; you by your father, me by my father."

"But you've done just what he wanted you to."

"I'm not what he wanted me to be," Harry cried passionately. "I'm not at all what he thinks I am, looking at me from the outside."

He looked at her reproachfully. "We're comrades too, Kate!"

She kissed him. "Against our fathers, who ruin it for everyone! Fuck 'em," she said and yawned.

"But don't get fucked," Harry whispered and fell asleep with his glass on his chest. Kate slipped the glass from his fingers and drew the sheet round his shoulders. Utterly worn out, she tucked her feet between his legs and went under.

Way, way under, the sounds of cannons reached her. There was a heavy weight on her chest and Kate thought stubbornly about pushing it off. It was imperative to get out of the trap, for the street was under siege. Doggedly, she concentrated on the task, but her arms caressed the weight like feathers. Her face was sticky with blood and itched horribly. It was so hot!

Kate Stevens sat up and Cam tumbled onto the bed into a patch of sun shaped by the window. Somberly regarding her daughter, cannons boomed in her head, boomed in memorial for the wasted morning.

"I stink," she informed her daughter. Unwholesome in heart and body, the lass lay reeking in the sun. Cam sat like Buddha, a felt-tip marker clutched in her hand. Ladders of saliva hung from her mouth as she colored Kate's breast blue. Silently, Kate observed the large, wobbly figures of Cam's fancy running up her arm.

"Good morning." Kate kissed the bright, hot head.

Then her stomach contracted and she vaulted over the child, flung open the bathroom door, and puked.

"Daa, daa!" A roman salute to the talented child, now seriously decking out the sheet. Catching sight of her wildly signed features in the bathroom mirror, Kate broke up. Leaping lines on her forehead and cheeks, dots on her chin and nose. They would come off, Kate hoped, or Margo would have a fit. Bleeding blue under the faucet, her hand came clean.

She filled the tub and stepped in, the smug mother of an imaginative child, then screamed at the sound of Harry erupting in the bedroom, followed by a loud smack. The ink would wash out, for Christ's sake!

"Stop slapping her!" Kate rose righteously, racing angry waves onto the floor.

In the doorway, Cam on his hip, Harry's haggard face was a shock.

"I slapped my own arm to scare her." The grave, dry-eyed baby bore no marks.

Gazing at his wretched face, Kate burst out: "You had horrible nightmares."

Sometime this morning she'd woken to find Harry groaning and moaning beside her, his arms like pipes in the air.

"You were having a terrible argument with someone, but you were totally out. Your eyelids were glued down. Who were you fighting with?"

He looked at her miserably.

"I don't remember." Going to the door, he told her that Mrs. Quinn had gone to the Bronx to nurse a sick cousin. "I'll feed Cam and put her down, then it's your show, OK?"

"Damn it," she snarled, "I've got to pose this afternoon."

His voice faintly shook. "I can't take Cam to the law school."

"Are you sick?" she demanded harshly, but he'd walked out.

Kate hunted for her jeans and boots and sweater and found them under the desk. The rough materials rasped on her skin, and her feet, as she shoved them into her boots, ached horribly.

Harry had pulled Cam's high chair to the kitchen table, where he sat watching her and nursing a beer. As Kate hobbled through the door, he got up and poured her a cup of coffee.

"Sit down, honey." He pulled out a chair. "Want an egg? Some toast?"

She looked at her face in the coffee, then jiggled the cup. "I wouldn't go down to Margo's if the opening weren't next week. She's so frantic, I just don't dare not show."

Harry stuck a piece of chicken in Cam's mouth and glumly sucked his finger.

"I'm not jealous of your career," Kate lied. He wouldn't look at her. "I'm no more involved with Margo than you are with your work."

Harry stared at her in amazement; his mouth opened and shut.

"I've never gotten your total attention and time," Kate said reasonably. "And now it's going to be a two-way street."

"You idiot," Harry croaked. "I don't love my career. I don't want to fuck my career."

"Fucking is important and I don't love Margo."

The phone rang. Kate's knees hit the edge of the table as she leaped up. A brown tongue of coffee flew out of the cup and dove for the floor. Mortified, Kate turned her back as she took up the receiver and crouched against the wall.

It was Margo, mean-voiced. "Will you get your ass down here and kindly not waste any more of my time and patience?"

"Sure." Kate said, "but I'll have to bring the baby with me. I'm pretty sure she'll sleep, though."

"Jeez, I'm down on my knees for my luck! Down on my knees! I expect you within the hour. Now move, sweetheart!"

Utterly surprised, Kate hung up the phone. Did Margo think that because they'd been to bed she'd established some rash power over her? Margo was stupid, then, and

176

way out of line. Shocked and contemptuous, Kate kept her back to Harry as she went to the high chair to take Cam down.

"No," Harry said softly, edging past, neither touching or looking. "I'll take her."

"You've got to go to work."

Cam high on his shoulder, Harry slightly bowed to her and smiled, so charming and assured, as though she were a stranger. "Don't trouble yourself."

Then, in his graceful, bounding way, he was out of the kitchen and beyond the living room before she had stepped into the hall.

Walking in the streets, waiting out the stops in the dreary subway stations, the slowly opening, closing doors, Kate's mood was imperative. But, above her mood, her mind clucked and disapproved.

The scene in the kitchen was bad, bad, bad. Her crashing legs, the spilled coffee. God, she should have explained, run around to Cam's room and described the space she was in. How Valery St. John, driving her from within, was not a rival to Harry but a goal for herself. If they'd talked, he would have understood that Kate could not have coolly turned in the kitchen, could not have said: "Fuck that rude bitch, I'll take Cam."

A wheel was whirling in her, the spokes a sheet of silver from the speed, and with her weathering face and stiffish body, she could only watch. Her face, flashing by in the black windows, lay over her callow lust like old paint. She grinned at it, gave it a wink. Dragged in the wake of her conception, panting, aching, jostled along – a tired old broad with an idea.

13

Kate pumped up the four flights of stairs to the loft door. The bolt shot angrily back. Kate's eyes traveled the slope of Margo's neckline and greeted her leisurely breasts – she dared not look at her face – with an uncontrolled smile.

Margo, silent, picked up a brush and paced between the work table and the canvas, then came over to the platform, as Kate pulled off her boots, and stood over her. The large knuckles of her sandaled feet, the no-nonsense, paint-splattered corduroys and the stony legs beneath, drew nervous chatter from Kate.

"I saw Elizabeth flying along the street – charging off to battle. She's really terrific, isn't she?" Kate moved edgily past Margo and climbed onto the platform. "Isn't it awful about – "

"Shut up."

"No," she cried, but really she was glad Margo had stopped her rash flow, no matter how rudely. She'd run into Elizabeth on the street in the bright, early morning, on her way to confer with Harry. She was exuberantly scornful of the administration.

"Willy Hay has been expelled!" She'd taken Kate's arm and pulled her along for a block. "Dean Bender must be in a state of panic. Why else would he have acted so stupidly?" She'd waved jauntily and strode on, leaving Kate to slowly walk back to the loft.

What would Harry say to her? Elizabeth was no pirate. Elizabeth had been beaten up too.

Kate's mind churned. Meeting her cousin had made something clear to her that she hadn't even dreamed. The previous night, Harry's rage at Willy Hay had been fortified, even inflamed, by the response of Kate's father. It had camouflaged the stark fact that Harry had made a deal with Dean Bender – that he'd sold out! So awful...

Margo moved back, her intense eyes telling Kate that the session had begun. Kate concentrated on the engines of the encircling lights, the tolerant, summer, humming sound filling up her consciousness, driving it inland, to a still, bright place.

Suddenly Margo flung her brush at Kate's legs and shouted:

"Get on your clothes and get out!" Margo rushed her, pulled her by the arm down two steps. Kate sat down on the third and crouched over her bare legs, her chest booming.

"I said, get out."

"No," Kate whispered. "I won't."

"Look at me, please!" The woman's bitter expression terrified Kate. "You and Elizabeth are a miserable pair. Spoiled, rich, namby-pamby babies! Having yourself an adventure, bless your puerile heart, getting yourself a little material for that novel that you'll finally be able to write." Margo sucked in her cheeks. "You smile? I ought to smack you."

Kate ducked. "It's nerves, Margo!"

179

"The day is shot, you little bitch! You got here so late we can't even begin. We've five days left! That's nothing for the work we have to do and you waltz in here chattering about the rally. Just like Elizabeth. She looks at the painting on the way out the door and says, 'Come on down to the law school, it'll do you good.'"

Margo put both hands in her hair and pulled. "The bloody, rotten gold dust twins have finished me!"

Kate slipped into her underpants and shirt and moused into the kitchen, where Margo, her head flung back, trumpeted a Scotch bottle. Roland was a woman, after all, and Kate saluted the dame who fell back against the fridge and belched.

Margo glowered at Kate's out-flung arm and snatched up a butcher's knife from the dish rack. "Frivolous little bitch!" She lowered the Scotch bottle. "I think I'll kill you."

Kate grabbed the bread board as ignoble laughter dribbled out of her. With her boots, jeans, and stout leather belt in the other room, there was no chance of conjuring up stern St. John valor. Hanging the bread board down her back, Kate made a dash for her costume. Margo suavely followed, the Scotch again at her lips and at her side a sword.

Struggling with the zipper, Kate jumped back as Margo made a grim pass at her breast.

"Stand still," the lady said, grinning, "I'll balance you up. You'll be the very image of the boy you've always longed to be – above the waist, that is. Is my little girl going to cry?"

"You shut up!"

Margo cocked her brows. Shouted: "But what else would a tomboy wish to be? The real thing has an irresistible draw to the unreal" – she flicked her cruel eyes at Kate's gaping zipper – "thing!"

Kate dragged on her boots and felt, beyond the clamor of automatic emotion, the presence of a strange peace, which grew steadily stronger as Margo railed.

"Whatever attracted Harry to our little phony boy? Her social position, her money? The gold dust twins! I'm so glad I thought of that. It's perfect for you and Elizabeth. Little, soft, gold-dusted babies! Miss Graves, you know, could live off the interest her money brings in. I'll be lucky if I ever make more than eight thousand a year."

Margo stalked to the painting and stood glaring up. "She sees that I work like a dog, day after day – she sees that, and yet she says, in that social way of hers, 'You must come to the rally, it will be so amusing.' Why, after all this time, does Elizabeth still think that my painting is some sort of therapy?"

Margo drank heartily from the bottle, the butcher's knife casually gripped. Her eyes, pulled wide with anger, never left the portrait of Kate. The face of her self-portrait, the gay, challenging face of a middle-aged tomboy, loomed over the brightly lit scene and Kate saw the tremendous effort in holding such an expression. For the face of the real Margo, was not, at the moment, drawn up to the fight, its sassy aggression drained away, the subtle mouth drooping, and sadness, as soft and formless as sand, the sadness of years sifted over the barricades of nose and chin.

Margo looked at the knife, then savagely skidded it across the yellow floor and into the dark beyond. "If I had any guts, I'd rip that huge fucker to shreds. If," – she choked and pressed her arm impatiently to her eyes –"if I had any guts" – she talked into her arm – "I'd slash the compulsive ass that paints – " She looked up at the canvas and then at Kate with huge, dark, frightened eyes.

"That ugly face! The chin looks like a buttered football and those are crazy, stupid eyes! You don't look like that, I dredge it up from my mud. Every time I paint I dredge it up!" She put the Scotch on the work table and stumbled off. "I'm sick," she groaned. "Going to bed. Go home."

The bedsprings creaked. Kate waited a moment, then went into the bedroom and cautiously approached the stricken warrior, flung out on her stomach. She slipped the old-fashioned quilt from beneath the painter's feet and, dropping it over her, respectfully tucked it around.

"Don't go," Margo whispered ...

"I won't." Kate sat down and began to stroke Margo's head and shoulders. Her scalp and back were cold and clammy and at the touch of Kate's hand Margo began to shiver.

"Keep touching me," she cried as Kate withdrew her hand.

"I just want to cover your feet." Kate carefully wrapped up the feet, kissed them, and went back to rubbing Margo's head and shoulders.

As the minutes went by, Kate felt Margo's anguish seeping cold through her palm and into her body. The panic tank stored in her own chest, never dry, flooded. Wonder Woman shot out of the sky by her own true love!

Could Elizabeth guess the effect of her remark? Did Margo often collapse like this, or was the cause the strain of the opening just five days away? Kate remembered Elizabeth's radiance in the street. Had she launched herself so high on the momentary wreck of her friend? And then Margo taking her pain and slamming it into Kate, calling her a phony boy. Christ, they were all on a shaky roadway across a swamp. Halfway across, don't look back, don't look down because guilt, Goddess of the amber pool, will hook you with her plaintive gaze and drown you in the muck of self-hatred and despair.

Margo is scared. Wonder Woman, my leader, lies gassed by the swamp fumes rising from her own soul. Kate drew back the blanket, then covered them both as she slipped down against Margo and hugged her fiercely.

Margo turned over and looked quietly up at Kate, "Ah, God, it's a bitch, isn't it?"

"I love your face." For the longest time Kate traced the strong, sad, face with her lips, pulling at Margo's depressed mouth, exploring her tongue and teeth. Her fingers in Margo's ears, sucking her nose, her chin, her nipples, Kate could not touch and smell enough.

"You're a genius, Kate! You've warmed me up and my God" – she slapped her stomach – "I've got to have something to eat."

Standing at the stove and cooking scrambled eggs, going back and forth to the fridge for butter and milk, Margo laughed incredulously. "You've got to stop following me around. I can't cook."

Kate hugged her round the waist and kissed her back. "I can't stop touching you. I love you madly; I love your blue shirt."

Margo took her by the shoulders and sat her at the kitchen table. "Now, hang onto this knife and butter the toast when it's ready."

After the meal Margo leaned back in her chair, stretched her long legs to the radiator, and drank brandy. "I feel so much better." She blew a kiss across the table.

"You're sweet, Kate Stevens, odd as they come, but sweet, very! God, I really do feel incredibly better. When Elizabeth swished out that door and I took a look at that buttered football I'd painted for a chin, I dropped a hundred miles. I could just hear the review: 'Margo Schwartz is as unskilled in the techniques of her art as she was ten years ago.'"

"You shouldn't care what the reviewers say."

"Elizabeth says that to me a lot and always, I've come to notice" – Margo tapped her head and looked clever – "always, just after she's knocked my work. In subtle ways, mind you, so subtle that I used to think she was simply mindful of my health and my total development as a human being."

She pushed the brandy bottle across the table. "Don't look so troubled, hon. Have another shot." She watched approvingly as Kate filled the small glass to the brim. "Elizabeth is always screaming that I load her down with guilt every time she goes through the door. So you see, it's a two-way street, sometimes very tough and cold, but, what the hell, that's life." Margo gestured jauntily and grinned. "I wonder if there's any time to – "

"I can't pose tonight," Kate interrupted. "I've got to get home."

"I've got to get home," Margo piped, "or Harry bear will eat me all up." She frowned and pouted. "'It's not fair,' she's thinking. 'I stand on a hot platform, hurting like hell day after day, and all I get is criticism.'"

Kate mastered herself. "That's somewhat true."

"You little sweetheart." Margo reached across the table and batted Kate's head. "Somewhat true, the little lady says, somewhat true? It's absolutely true. Face it, baby, you're letting yourself be used, but not really, because we both know you've got a sleeveful of tricks, a sleeve just bulging with politics, a most political sleeve."

Margo loped round the table and dropped a smacking kiss on Kate's head. "Oh, don't pout, it's all fine, in fact, it's all terrific. You're an adventurer, my darling. So is Elizabeth and so am I."

"You were very, very sweet to me just when I needed it most. Of course, I shouldn't let Elizabeth push me out of planes without a parachute, but life" – she extravagantly kissed the air – "is an education in itself."

She leaned forward, foot saucily cocked. "Hark! A key in the lock, a lock in the door, a door in the wall, and through it marches my own true love."

Margo marched smartly around the table, then gallantly bowed Elizabeth through the kitchen door. "How goes the revolution?"

Elizabeth gave Kate and Margo a bleak smile and sat down at the kitchen table.

"Hello, bitches!"

From behind her, Harry quietly appeared in the small kitchen, and Margo, startled, stared hostilely, causing him to color slightly and step back into the doorway.

"Make some tea, Harry," said Elizabeth in a tone that told Margo not to be an ass.

His head down, Harry went past Margo to the stove, filled the kettle, and put it on the heat.

"I could use some," Margo said aggressively to Harry's back. "What the hell's going on? Are you two having an affair?"

Kate opened the cupboard and got down the cups. She put a tea bag in each and reached across Harry, her face hot as she took hold of the handle, for he'd shied at the touch of her arm as if she were a leper.

"I'm just about the last man in the world Elizabeth would have an affair with, I'm sad to say."

Margo turned round the chair and straddled it with a flash of her long leg. She put her arms across the back and supported her unsmiling face.

"Well, just don't try to prove that."

With a charming laugh, Harry sat down opposite her and held up his hand, palm out. "Scout's honor."

"I joined the girl scouts because I was mad to wear the uniform. I still have my knife with the can opener and the corkscrew and the big and little blades."

Harry gulped his tea noisily while Margo's sugary-sweet voiced flowed over his bent head. His face flamed and eyes flooded. "Hot," he gasped.

"Mustn't be greedy," she purred. Elizabeth glared from beneath her bangs.

"Why don't you and Kate go – *paint!*"

A droplet of saliva flew across the table and collided with Margo's forehead.

"Really, darling, you don't have to be so – personal." She wiped her brow with the back of her hand. "I don't happen to want to paint at the moment. In fact, I'm just dying to hear the news from the front and I'm sure that Kate is just as anxious as I."

Kate found herself bending forward and giving Elizabeth a polite smile.

"You'll be glad to know, Margo, that my political days are over!" Margo looked totally unfazed by the accusation in Elizabeth's spiteful tone.

"Why don't you tell Margo what a shit I am?" Harry gazed steadily across the table at the top of Elizabeth's head with eyes that were philosophical and melancholy.

"I'm all ears," Margo exclaimed.

"You don't care, Margo, so don't pretend you do!"

Elizabeth's combative look drew a smile from Margo. "What happened, Liz? Did the rally fizzle?"

"There wasn't any rally," Elizabeth shouted. Margo ducked behind her hands. "Not so loud, not so loud!"

"Elizabeth is furious at me because I called the rally off." Harry reached across the table with his big hand and gently raised her chin.

"No!" Elizabeth wrenched her head away and stood. Kate was startled to see the Crazy Jane face that Margo had painted, the bright, glazed, troubled eyes. "I can't bear the dean's meanness. He knows he's lost, he's decided to go, but not without revenging himself! The rally would have paid him back, made him miserable – oh, God, he's such a petty little shit!"

Harry finished his tea and stood up. "I keep telling you he's not important."

"You keep telling her?" Margo jeered. "That'll be the day!"

"Well, I am too emotional, too personal." Elizabeth walked behind Margo and put her hands on her shoulders. "But I boil when I think of what the dean has done." She nodded at Harry. "I know you're being sensible. We've got what we want and Willy Hay is no saint."

"Baloney!" Margo shouted. She smiled sweetly up at Elizabeth, "It's time you got off your high horse and realized that you're no better than the rest of us scum."

Harry laughed in a pained and violent way as he went out the door. "That's right, Graves! Join the human race!"

Kate drooped down the four flights of stairs after Harry and lolled beside him in the cab, miserable beyond words.

She hated Harry's tired, depressed face and snarled: "You gave the driver the wrong address." He flipped up the collar of his raincoat and turned his shoulder to her.

"You're forgetting, darling. We've got to pick up Cam."

And all the way uptown from that narrow street, that narrow house near the law school, Harry looked down at the child in his lap, who sucked on the bottle and slept with her tiny bunch of fingers curled round his thumb.

Violently ashamed that she'd forgotten to ask the whereabouts of her daughter, Kate was sick at sea, very, very sick.

Harry would not let her hold Cam even when he needed both hands to find his wallet, and later, at the door of the apartment – Kate extended her arms for the child and slowly let them drop – he managed the key, the unlocking, with Cam asleep on his chest. But the plastic bottle fell through his arm. Kate picked it off the rug, washed it carefully, and filled it with warm milk.

In Cam's bedroom Kate didn't try to give the bottle directly to Cam, didn't try to kiss the child as Harry gave her the bottle, but dragged off to the bathroom, where she washed her hair and cried briefly under the heavy water.

When Kate came out of the bathroom, the slit of light, before she clicked it off, showed Harry lying on his side at the very edge of the bed.

Kate crept under the covers. "Elizabeth is in love with you." The bulk of his back and shoulders, although hostile, was still a comfort. When she realized that she would sleep, Kate reached out and touched his back.

"If Elizabeth loves you – you can't be all bad."

His arm flew up; the lamp crashed to the floor. Harry loomed, his hands closing round her neck. See his big, blond head. Hear him sob. Kate relaxed in his tough grip. Physical pain was a breeze.

"Good," she kept thinking, ''I'm so glad." Then Harry took his hands from her throat, picked the lamp off the floor, and turned it on.

Kate sat up, breathing like mad. "Think you're such a fucking big deal!" He turned away, his face utterly miserable.

"Oh, Harry! What have you done? What is going on?" She pulled on his shoulders.

He shook her off, going round the bed and sitting at the far corner, where she couldn't reach him. Over the long ridge of his shoulder he gloomily announced: "I could go to bed with Elizabeth anytime I wanted."

Kate fitted a pillow to the back of her head and pulled the sheet up to her chin.

"She thinks I'm a great guy." He squinted at her.

"I know she does. That's not what I'm talking about."

"She trusts my judgment about Willy Hay."

189

"So you're a judge now? You mean that she agrees you've got bigger fish to fry."

He turned round and looked at her accusingly. "She thinks I'm an idealist no matter what I do!"

"That's sweet."

"You bitch!" His head turned heavily away. She listened to him breathe and watched the thick artery in his neck thud with blood. Cam cried out. Kate swung her legs from beneath the covers. Harry caught her ankle and held her. "Where you going?"

"Cam's crying."

"You're hearing things," he said, then started up himself at the baby's loud wail. Before leaving the room, she looked up at him, almost asleep. With his hands on his hips, he stood mournfully in the doorway.

"When I was ten, I hated people like Dean Bender. When Cam is ten, she'll hate me!"

"You need to get back on the track," she shouted at his back. The snap of a switch and light breaking in the narrow hall, his soft, cajoling voice and Cam's loud, gay sounds constituted, Kate felt, his agreeing answer. There was no doubt that Cam would love him always, the way she loved Margo; in her ears, in her nose, in her stomach, in her skin – the rest would follow.

14

Each night when she got home from Margo's, Kate found Harry pronged between earphones and flooded with Scotch. Felled on the rug in his underclothes, the silently spinning records spoke secrets to his floating brain. The Scotch bottle wedged in his armpit, he'd open his green eyes at her nudge, but not his mouth. In the mornings he'd vomit, shave, and eat a banana on the street to the subway.

Kate hung out the window, called down to her swiftly striding husband: "We must talk."

His fist went up, his large fingers opening. "Right on!"

A rotten week. Kate Stevens, bullied by Margo and ignored by her husband, has achieved her ambition. Every afternoon at dusk she is commanded to the pleasures of the painter's ravenous flesh. This constitutes their two-hour break, after which Margo orders Kate back to the platform to stand until midnight. To get herself through, Margo sniffs speed through a stumpy straw. It doesn't occur to the artist to offer her model a snort, no doubt because Kate is an uptight, body-blind WASP. And yet, while fucking, the arrogant lady would order Kate back to the shower so that she might continue her coolie labors with a fresh hide.

Stepping back into her footprints on the blue felt platform, Kate sniffed the smell of Margo still on her fingers and mulled.

An utterly absurd woman! An absurd passion! On her feet, Margo struts, whirls, swoops, and glides until Kate aches for that energy. Wheeling, pouncing, she battles the gross shapes, the ugly strokes that mock her fierce intention, until sweat flattens her hair to her head and gleams on her face and chest. Oh, oh, oh, to be loved by a dame so epic and true!

Later, strewn on Margo's still, lush form, Kate whispered: "Did you know that I've been fucking you since I've been ten?"

Margo shakes Kate off and does a slow turn on the red rug. "Get going, will you?" Which meant that Kate was to rub Margo's back until the tension left her shoulders and neck. As each day brought Margo closer to the opening, closer too, Margo was sure, to a breakup with Elizabeth.

"She's not even a fuck anymore," the painter groaned, "she's just a person."

Each morning the face that peered past the heavy steel door grew darker. With sharkish malice, she always asked: "And how is handsome Harry this morning?" Had Kate cooked his favorite breakfast, had she polished up his huge purple shoes?

Then she'd stamp around the narrow kitchen while Kate made coffee. Since the beginning of the week, Elizabeth had come home to sleep, change her clothes, and that was it, baby. What little she said was Harry this and Harry that, Harry the bold, the wise, the beautiful!

"She thinks their damned committee is going to turn

the law school into the garden of Eden. She's writing memos on the student interviews that she conducts twenty-four hours a day and she's sublimely sure that whatever everyone wants, Lord Harry will grant."

She made an agonized face over Kate's shoulder. "Please tell me what turns a rational toughie into a drippy cunt? I know, of course. It's the excuse to paint up one's masochism as the love of a great man. Did you know you were married to a great man?" Margo sagged against Kate. "I wonder if they've fucked. Naw, they're both too namby-pamby."

Kate described Harry's nightly stupor between the earphones and said that Margo was shooting wild.

"But where is he shooting? That's what I want to know."

Kate poured out the coffee, pointing out the cup to Margo, who stared bleakly into the sink. "Elizabeth's trying to make you jealous. If she were involved with Harry, she wouldn't mention him at all."

That morning and afternoon Margo worked to a state of exhaustion, then lay like a zombie on the red rug, fuming at Kate's incompetence – she was as unskilled as Elizabeth, for Christ's sake, who was the worst lay in town! Finally, slapping her hands on Kate's bottom like big, broken fins, Margo moaned: "Here it comes, almost here, yes, yes, almost here, oh, don't stop now, don't stop!"

Kate jabbed Margo's box with her knee as she flopped onto the rug.

"Hey, cowboy, what's the matter with you?"

"That's fantasy sex," Kate shouted.

"Look at you, all red in the face and shuffling about in

my jeans. I feel better. I wonder if there's enough time – "

"You're incredible! I can hardly stand."

Margo pulled her down. "Then, sit, have a drink. A smoke? No? Dear, dear, what's up with him?"

Kate swung round on her knees and slapped Margo across the face. "I'm not a man! I don't have a cock! You're obscene."

Margo slapped her neatly back. "And you, my sweet, are a bang, bang, banging boy. You don't really think that women make love like that?" She smiled knowingly. "You even hit like a boy. Fantasy sex, my ass! Where do you get off? That's not my style. Intriguing, I admit, but not my style."

Kate watched Margo with sullen caution. "Then, what is your style?" With a wink and a cavalier swing of her hips, Margo went off to the bathroom. Kate flopped down on the red rug, her nose deep in the dusty pile. In the beginning she thought there was the word, announcing the great reality. But for Margo there was only one word, the whole ball game was her word: her stubborn, lying pride that on her feet and on her ass she is the swashbuckling, thrill-a-minute, dynamo lover. Time after time, it was Kate all over her, panting, pumping, into her everywhere – and then Margo would invariably have the nerve to say, her voice so calm and deep, "I want to make love to you."

Kate jumped up, opened the bathroom door, and addressed the rattling shower curtain. "But you've never made love to me, Margo."

A considering sigh.

"I was all set to jump on your bones yesterday but you ran away to the john."

194

"And when I raced back, you were out cold."

"Was I? Oh, the poor lamb."

"You're just using me," Kate stormed. "I'm going home."

The shower curtain whipped back. "But we use each other, darling." Margo held out her arm for a towel. Kate hesitated, then tossed it to her.

"You could bang away for another year and not get it all out. Indeed, you shouldn't want to get it out, it's very exciting to feel such intensity. You're quite right that I use you. I relax and fill up with your force. It gives me the confidence I need to keep painting." She looked in the mirror. "To tell you the truth, honey, these are bad days for me. I just don't think I could make love to a sweet, young chick."

Kate put her arms around Margo's wet waist and hugged her hard. "You're the best person in the world."

They both looked into the mirror. "I'm ugly and old and I don't give a shit."

Kate smiled and kissed Margo's shoulder. "You've a great face."

"You're out of your mind, love." Her eyes met Kate's cheerfully. "Still, it wasn't a bad facade before it all fell in."

Kate reached for her jeans. "Shall I get the door?"

Margo swept up. "Why, darling?"

"Someone's knocking at the door."

Margo loped off between the lights and disappeared in the darkness at the far end of the loft.

Kate heard Harry's humorous, drunken drawl and jumped for her jeans and shirt, her arms and legs snagging in the material.

He stepped into the circle of light and greeted her with a bow.

"Knock off for a bit and I'll buy you both dinner." He drew a flat bottle from his raincoat pocket and gaily drank, tossing the hair out of his eyes.

Margo grabbed his wrist and pulled him in front of the painting.

"Wait," he cried, rocking Margo like a football buddy. "I need food first, platters and platters of delicious Chinese food."

Margo knocked him with her elbow. "He looks at the greatest painting of the century and thinks of bean sprouts."

"Fried pork, lobster Cantonese, duckling with pineapple, and those juicy, black mushrooms." He kissed the top of her head. "Dress, woman."

Margo watched his delighted, cruising eyes and with a proud smile threw back her shoulders.

Banging down from the platform, Kate sourly announced that she would not, after drinking and eating, go back to work.

"Of course not! We're going to have fun." Margo pushed Kate into the bathroom, then, whistling and singing in croaky spurts, she got out the ice and settled Harry with a drink. When Kate came into the bedroom she found her costume for the evening laid out across the bed. As Margo showered for the second time in an hour, Kate drew on a pair of soft brown wool trousers and a white silk blouse with billowing sleeves that fastened tightly at the wrist.

Margo swept down in black bikini pants. "No, no,

silly." She tugged out the shirt that Kate had so carefully tucked in. "It's worn outside the pants and belted."

Kate stood like a lump as Margo drew a tangle of belts from the bureau drawer. Arms above her head as she worked a belt free, her strong body arched back and braced on a solid leg, Margo shot her a proud, happy smile. She presented a tableaux of dramatic, graceful poses as she dressed. Gray silk shirt and soft, pale gray velvet trousers. She slipped on a pair of short black patent-leather boots, then smiled down at her nimble, shiny feet as she danced round the bed.

In front of the mirror, swaying softly before her image, Margo lit a joint and passed it amiably to Kate. Amiable, easy, she armed her fingers with pewter rings, brushed her hair, and drew her thirties eyebrows. It was all so simple. They'd worked like hell and now they deserved some fun. And yet, when Margo turned from the mirror to give Kate a final check, the young woman was cold as ice and pitched to the bottom of a dark well.

"Idiot, the belt doesn't go round your waist." She bent and worked the belt down on Kate's hips. "What's the matter, honey?" she asked.

Kate shook her head, unable to speak. Moving back into the kitchen, Harry stood to greet her, a huge, blond man with an open respectful face.

On the street, the artist took Harry's arm as they walked to the restaurant, with Kate dragging behind. Margo tipped up the brim of her black Spanish hat, hitched up her shoulders, and managed with her audacious swagger and low laugh to be football buddies with Harry, old pals out on a binge. And who, Kate wondered, would

197

hold the door? Two doors. How easily they managed. Margo ushered Harry through the first, who stepped back and held the inner door for Kate. Oh, my! Two such handsomes!

The booths, explained the hostess, were for parties of six and they, her almond eyes clicked on each, were only three.

Margo pushed back her hat and explained that Harry was twice the size of a normal man and that she, being the equal of two normal women, made them a party of four, and adding this one, she pulled over Kate, made them five.

Her delicate brown hand covering her mouth, the Chinese woman giggled. "You are two and he is two but," she glanced mischievously at Kate, "she is only one."

The hostess led them to a booth, where they slid across the red plastic cushions as Margo directed, first Kate, then Harry beside her. She'd forgotten her cigarettes and was off down the aisle before Harry could dig out his pack.

"Order me a martini," she called.

Harry turned to watch her. "Does your friend know that her shirt is open to her waist? The cashier doesn't know where to look. Neither do I."

She kicked him. "Liar!"

They both laughed.

"What are you two giggling about?" Margo slid into the booth and in the sudden loop of her shirt, two brown breasts hung at their ease. "No drinks?" She peered around muttering. "Let's get partying here!"

Harry studied the menu, his stomach gurgling so loudly that Margo laughed. "We'll order food with the drinks. You're starving."

Harry passed over the menu and asked if Margo would order for him. Kate sputtered. He never let *her* order for him.

"Margo knows about Chinese food."

"How do you know?"

Margo laughed. "I do, actually."

Two drinks later the food arrived. Margo's big, cracked fingers curled round the stem of her martini, her hat angled so that she regarded them from a strip of shadow thrown down by the brim, Margo directed the waiter to serve Harry first while she explained to him her particular system of sauces. But the pile of chicken and vegetables was excavated by Harry's madly moving fork and spoon before Margo's system could be applied and she looked at the boy in astonishment.

"Elizabeth eats like that." She clicked her front teeth like castanets. "Her digestion is lousy because she thinks she can do without the slow, grinding movement of her molars."

Harry reached into his coat pocket and handed Margo two sheets of paper stapled at the corner.

"I want to talk to you about this." He helped himself to steak in oyster sauce and lobster triple crown. He poured out tea and ate his food with relish as Margo threw a glance over the paperwork. Kate pretended to ignore this apparently exclusive consultation, fuming.

Silverware jangled as Margo read through the paperwork cursorily. "When did she find out her course was being dropped?" Her pleasant, casual tone belied the hostile suspicion that showed in her face.

"She got a notice from the committee this morning."

Harry took off his glasses, his eyelids blinking furiously as his hand came up to his face. His lips pulled upward as his fingers dug into his sockets and rubbed.

"What committee, darling?"

"It's a handful of older faculty members who decide who teaches what and when."

Kate shivered.

"What did the notice say?"

Harry adopted a formal, wry tone. "I don't recall the words, but the substance of it was that Elizabeth's highly popular seminar entitled 'Women, the Family, and the Law' would not be given next semester. Instead, she was to devote her talents to the much neglected (some think deservedly neglected) area of maritime law."

"Maritime law? That couldn't draw so much as a bathtub of interest. Anyway, what does Elizabeth know about that?"

"Well, as it states in this announcement you're reading, Elizabeth knows nothing at all about that. She is therefore appealing over the head of the committee directly to the student body."

Kate whistled softly. "She's right!"

Harry raised his big hand as though to block Kate out. "Of course, Elizabeth is right. I question her tactics."

"Oh, God!" Kate hooted and was hurt and surprised by Margo's irritated response.

"Elizabeth is exposing herself before she's lined up any support," he said.

"Won't the students support her?"

"Nobody on that committee gives a damn what the students think or feel or do. Elizabeth could unroll a petition a hundred miles long and all those guys would see in it is that Miss Graves is more dangerous than they thought."

"Ah, they're full of shit." Margo sneered. "Go down fighting, what the hell!"

Harry gave a shout of humorless laughter, a sort of despairing bray. He had come down to see her, hoping that Margo's contempt for politics would aid him in dealing with Elizabeth. He'd hoped that Margo would agree that the petition was an act of senseless, political sacrifice.

"If she antagonizes the committee by appealing directly to the students, her career will be over!"

"Did you tell her that?" Margo lifted off her hat and placed it beside her on the seat.

"I told her that she'd be teaching maritime law for the rest of her life."

In Harry's face and voice, ever so faint but newly there, Kate recognized her father's bullying way of taking reality into his fist and pounding one to death with *the way things were*.

"You bum!" Kate shouted.

Margo shook her finger at Kate. "Don't be rude, darling." Kate was appalled at the sweet smile Margo shot across the table at her husband. "You must talk to her again, Harry! She'll listen. She thinks you're a great man."

Kate pounded the table. "He has nothing to say to Elizabeth because he's sold out!"

Margo reached over her plate and downed the last of Kate's martini. "For once in your life, baby, live a little time without that independent income of yours and then you can talk about selling out!"

Kate stood, slipped Margo's hat under her, and sat down on it hard.

"You bitch!"

Kate pointed at Harry. "I've married my fucking father."

She hated him so. His huge, softly breathing hulk, his hands peeling off bills, the arrogant way he signaled the waiter and the way he could completely ignore her. Out loud, in his easy, pleasant voice, he figured the tip. He put his wallet back in his pocket, then stood, looking up at the ceiling and straightening his tie. Because he was a big, blond man, his deepest sense of himself was sleek and approving. His conscience was covered with heavy oil.

"You're rotten with ambition," she said.

He looked smoothly down. "You're full of shit."

"I want my hat," Margo snapped. Kate stood and sat down again.

"Talk about a sell-out! You lousy, rotten bitch, agreeing with him!"

Margo looked incredulously from Harry to Kate. "Your scene is too much. Why am I involved in this? Where is my hat?" She tugged it out from beneath Kate, her fingers plucking at the crumpled crown. "I've never known anyone to deliberately sit on a hat. What an incredibly childish thing to do."

On the street, arm in arm with Harry, Margo kept turning around and holding out her hand but Kate, slouched and sullen, hung behind. Passers by, pale in the light of the streetlamps and store windows, floated past.

Kate started to cross the street, her loathing eyes riveted on Margo, who was posed like a model on the curb, laughing up at Harry. A long horn blast blew her up and dropped her down. Yellow slid by and Kate kicked out as hard as she could. The taxi bounced to a stop. The driver opened the door on his side and peered at Kate over the roof of his cab.

"Did *you* kick my fender?"

Kate gave him the finger.

"What?"

She repeated the age-old gesture and spat in the street. The cab headlight lit his bulk as he dashed at her. His hands locked on her arm and he dragged her over to the cab.

"See what you did?"

She peered with surprise at a respectable dent and turned away from his sharp breath. As he bent over her, his face, as cratered as the moon, filled with greenish lamplight.

He shook her violently. "You're going to pay for that."

"Pockmarked fuck!"

"What?"

Kate aimed for his groin but her knee misfired and cracked against his. She butted with her head, threw a punch, then was groined to the sidewalk, her mouth stretching round strange, deep, hoarse noises.

Back to the scene she came, curled on the pavement, tight as a nighttime flower. She crawled to the gutter and vomited as Harry bribed the driver. Then she became a foul scarf for his neck as he swept her up and across his shoulders. The strong, vigorous rhythm of his step mocked her felled frame and she began to wail.

"Shut up," cried Harry.

"Shut up," cried Margo.

Kate howled louder.

Harry shifted to a trot. His quick, hard step tapped cold sounds from her conquered interior.

The mustard stairwell funneled past. Margo closed and bolted the steel door. Easing Kate off his shoulders, Harry wanted to know if she could stand. His voice was too cold, she would not answer.

"Kate, honey, can you stand?"

Not being a medico under fire, she thought, he could take that tense, perfunctory "honey" and go fuck himself.

Margo turned on lights, brought out a pillow and blanket.

"Settle that poor child on the couch." Her attention was not in her hands and eyes as she tucked Kate in, but with Harry in the kitchen cracking out ice.

He handed Margo a drink, then put his cold hand on Kate's forehead.

"If you don't tell me how you feel, I'm going to call the doctor."

"Don't you dare."

"Then, let me see where he hit you."

Margo unbuckled Kate's belt and pulled up the shirt. "Poor darling," she crooned, but her fingers didn't linger, didn't care.

"It's just a bruise," Kate snarled. "Leave me alone."

Harry crouched. "Does it hurt?"

"Of course it hurts, you son of a bitch."

Margo grinned. "She's cursing – she can't be dying."

Out-run, out-jump, out-shoot, out-hit! Kate glared up at them. How could she be dying? She was simply dead.

She lay on her side away from them, her face pressed into the pillow.

Harry and Margo sat nearby, the glass-topped table between their chairs clinking intimately as they set down their drinks.

Middling to heavy drunk, Harry was off on his own track. "She'd have done better with that pig if she'd kept her guard up. Christ, she stood there like an open door. I thought she knew better."

"Why would she know better?"

A shuffling sound. "Like this, you know. Never let your left drop."

"Never?" Margo flirted.

"Never! She must have been drunker than I thought – to forgot the basic thing."

"Did you really teach Kate to box?"

"We've sparred around a lot. She's very fast – of course she doesn't have the strength, but if you've got the technique, you can hold your own, especially with all these light, little city men."

"Good god!"

"What's the matter?"

"One of you has really got to remember that Kate is not a man."

Harry was stalwart. "There are lots of men she could lick."

"Now, look here" – Margo laughed "with her guard up and a left hook and a right jab, Kate baby will be picking fights all over town. And you won't always be around to bail her out."

"Kate's not aggressive."

"Not aggressive? The girl who just kicked the tail of a cab with her boots, who attacked a cab driver with naked fists?" Margo laughed delightedly, then said in a coy voice that made Kate ashamed for her, "You promised to look at the painting after platters of Chinese food. Well?"

Kate heard the hum of the painting lights and slowly raised herself to stare over the top of the couch. As he looked, Harry grew crimson in the face and neck. Margo watched him tensely.

"What?" she asked as Harry dropped his head.

"I said, she's never looked that way with me."

Margo stepped up to him and put her hand on his shoulder. Harry got his glasses out of his coat pocket and gazed at the canvas again.

"Where is she going?"

"To seek her fortune." She planted a friendly kiss on his cheek, then stepped up to the canvas and brushed her fingers across the skillfully painted scar. "She went a few steps down to Hades, but she came back and she's moving on." She gestured blithely to the ceiling. "That's no threat, you know. That had to be."

"She's handsome, isn't she?"

"It should be better between you now, more fun."

Harry looked mournfully at the painting. "She's left me."

"Not if you keep up." Margo briskly patted his shoulder. "Keep up, keep up."

"I'm just a dumb southern boy, ma'am. I've gone about as far as I can go." Margo grinned and playfully kissed his mouth, her snaky tongue so quick and subtle.

Harry grabbed her. She slipped away, turned off

the painting lights, and then casually took his hand. Kate ducked.

"She's asleep," Margo whispered as they passed by.

Dragging the blanket behind her, Kate slipped off the couch, crawled across the floor to the bedroom doorway, and drew the blanket round her shoulders. She hears, and in her mind's eye, can see it all.

The lamp on the bureau sweetly lights the small space. Harry sits on the bed and bends to untie his shoes. Margo kneels behind him and kisses his neck. His eyes are blurry from the spicy fragrance that streams from between her breasts. Watch it, Harry baby, the old whore squirts it there, dead center, from a large bottle of perfume that she keeps in her bedside drawer.

A goner. Soft, moth eyes. Thick in the lip, he swallows like a rube. Kate threw back the blanket and straddled the wooden chair just outside the doorway, her hands tightly gripping the slats.

The scene is on tracks. Intensity blares its right to rule and, at the same time, is innocent in the gentle light from the bureau, and calm, like a child's room. Margo takes off her shirt and trousers, folds them neatly. She stretches out behind Harry's curved back and clasps her hands behind her head. Harry stands and pulls off his trousers, throws them in the corner. Margo casually beckons to him and sits. He comes and stands between her long, smooth legs.

Kate sits and mourns. Her harbor, her beach.

Something so simple and companionable about Margo, the way she slips off his oxford blue shorts and then looks at him with a little grin as if they are both to be congratulated. Harry grips her shoulders and pushes her back. His huge knees and elbows staple her narrow form and he tries to move in immediately.

"We've got all night, hon!" Groaning, Margo raises them both, then collapses with a sharp cry.

Crack! Kate looks down at the back of the chair, floating in her hands, detached from the base the force of her tension.

She thought of a tall, glistening person putting on a lavender shirt. Belting a pair of soft, dark trousers. When the painter feels lustful she simply lies down on the bed or floor and unzips her jeans.

When she has had enough, she shakes free, showers, nibbles from a bowl of cold rice, and goes about her work. Her simplicity is hard for the young woman to take, for in space and time, her body is a monument to be worshiped. Margo is no worshiper but a child beckoning with a bright face. Adventure, pleasure, oh, why not? Crawl through that hedge, lie with me, put your hand there. Oh, lovely!

Harry and Margo sit side by side on the bed, their legs touching in the gentle light. Harry smiles shyly and stretches out on his back at Margo's request. She slides down between his legs.

Kate paced outside the door, muttering, "I hope they both have heart attacks ..." Harry must be pulp, she thought. That's not desire I'm witnessing, but genital agony. Eeeeh! "Caught in the terrible dyke machine." The young woman could stand it no longer, yet could not leave. Christ, the noise! Floor, bedsprings, pants, whistles, groans. Margo had never put it out like that for her.

Kate was quite calm when the two peeled apart. "You don't waste your precious energies on women," she would never, not in a million years, dare say.

When Kate heard the shower running she threw herself down beside Harry.

"Now you're in love with Margo!"

He lay like a log, his eyes fixed on the ceiling. "What's the matter?"

"I'm poisoned," he whispered. "Ending."

"You're just beginning," she bitterly said.

His arm swung out, knocking her off the bed. "I don't like sleeping with whores in front of my wife," he whispered.

She leaped up. "Who made you?"

"You did, bitch! I loved our life before!" He gathered up his clothes, crying as he dressed himself. When Harry had wept over his older brother, buried in his father's backyard, Kate had wept too, but now she watched her husband cautiously, heard the accusation of his deep emotion, and drew back in terror.

"Our life isn't over," she said.

He slammed the bed. "Monkey tricks!"

Kate gestured despairingly. "Then, why?"

"I thought I could be a swinger like you."

She stamped her foot. "I'm not a swinger!"

His gay, striped tie whirled round as he tied the knot. He turned his back, adjusting his jacket on his shoulders as he went through the door.

15

Kate sat, stultified, in the bedroom, half listening to Margo cursing at an empty bottle on the kitchen table. It sounded distant, feeble, until she was jolted suddenly alive by the shock of an exuberant voice in the hallway.

"For heaven's sake, Margo, put your shirt on! Harry's here!"

Margo came through the bedroom door. She picked a candy-cane-striped shirt off the closet door and slipped into it, grinning.

"Come watch," she whispered to Kate. Watch me, watch me grinned the shark, before the water thickens and obscures the view ...

Elizabeth and Harry stood talking by the front door, Harry reaching for the bolt behind him as he looked into Elizabeth's excited face.

"Did you like my memo?"

He smiled, but looked away. "Yes, I liked it very much!"

Margo swiftly herded the two from the door toward the yellow cushioned chairs that she and Harry had left just an hour before. She fetched Kate from the bedroom, sitting the sullen young woman on the couch. Elizabeth paced between the chairs and couch and would not, when

Margo asked, take off her raincoat. She said she was cold. But the look of the raincoat was unbecoming, complained the painter, for what was, after all, a reunion.

As Elizabeth paced on, Margo jumped up and slung her arm around her shoulders.

"How's yourself?" She kept step, turning neatly at the edge of the red rug. "You do look smashing in your raincoat and boots. Did you do it?"

Elizabeth shook back her thick bangs and hugged Margo, laughing.

"Yes," she shouted, leaning back in the painter's arms. "I slipped my little protest in every mailbox in the law school lounge."

Margo drew a cheerful finger across her throat. "Have yourself a drink."

Elizabeth sat and stretched out her long, booted legs. "I'm already drunk," her bold, pure voice announced. "I feel marvelous!"

"Ah, the elation of self-sacrifice," Margo purred, as she sat in the nearby chair.

"Isn't she funny?" Elizabeth grinned at Harry, then reached for Margo's hand. "You're very funny, honey." Margo rolled her eyes. "I wonder where we'll be living next week."

"You don't understand, Margo Schwartz! You're a painter. You work like a dog to translate your ideas into images and you do beautiful work – beautiful work! The portrait of Kate should really put you on the map – the expression in the eyes, the mood of the whole thing is marvelous!" She leaned across the glass table and kissed Margo's pleased and surprised face.

"But you don't understand my thing, not at all!" Elizabeth gestured with affection at Harry. "My job is safe as long as that man over there is with me."

It seemed to Kate that the line of Harry's profile had hardened with arrogance. He'd slept with Margo right in front of her, had driven into her lover with a blind, proprietary lust, and then called the painter a whore. A whore, he'd said.

Margo gave him a quick, wry look. "He isn't God, you know."

"You're so silly, Margo! He doesn't need to be God."

Zeus listening with half an ear while the women chattered.

"I'm saying that you'd be safer if he were God."

"How safe do I need to be?" Elizabeth innocently asked.

Sharpening his thunderbolts while the women chattered.

"Safer than you are," Margo said blackly. "By far."

Gallant in her long boots and English raincoat, Elizabeth had sweated it out on the front lines, while the young punk general lived to see another day.

Kate hated him! Three cheers for Margo, who'd pulled the coward back from the door.

"I tell you, Margo! I'm so bored with your drunk, stoned, cynical view of life. I can't bear it anymore. You're just like one of those horrible turtles that swim up to the surface, bite into a duck's leg, and drag it drowning to the bottom. You don't want to think that good things can be accomplished! You're low!"

Margo shut Kate up with a friendly wave. "You leap to that opinion of me, but never mind. Can I ask you one thing before I pack up and clear out?"

Elizabeth impatiently brushed back her bangs. "Of course!"

"How do you explain the fact that the administration dared to expel Willy Hay?"

Elizabeth looked openly at Margo, the corners of her mouth glistening with saliva, like a child's.

His eyes flicking from Margo to Elizabeth, Kate watched the professor observing with amusement the two freaks carrying on. Yet he'd groaned like a baby under Margo. Kate pulled his sleeve.

"Christ, you'll never stop smiling, will you? You smile as if this was all beneath you, but you came here tonight to persuade Margo to stop Elizabeth. You don't dare talk to her yourself"

"He knows the score," Margo said coolly. "That's why he's smiling."

"You shut up. I pay the rent here. You haven't earned a penny in months."

Margo smiled agreeably: 'I'm living with Fort Knox, why the hell should I?"

"Get out." Elizabeth stamped her foot. "Get out of my life."

Margo mockingly stamped her foot. "At this moment I'm very cynical indeed, and I see no reason not to be."

She held her hands up calmly in the air. "Two facts to fret your interpretative faculties. The first, known to you, is that the administration dared to expel Willy Hay. The second, just revealed by Kate, is that Professor Stevens here, your hero, made a special trip down here tonight so that I might help him in talking you out of sending off your protest."

Exhausted, not tough, Harry slumped in his chair. Elizabeth kneeled before him, her hand resting on his knee.

"Why?" she whispered.

"You will lose your job, honey. I can't protect you."

"But why, if you're dean?"

He looked bleakly into her eyes. "Like Margo said – I'm not God."

"Well, don't brood about it," Margo teased. "Deity isn't essential here. Being a man will suffice."

Harry smiled dully, then got up, unsteady and lumbered off, knocking against the table, then the chair. Elizabeth went after him and took his arm.

"I'm sorry." He pulled away. "I'm sick, got to get home." Walking through the painting lights, he found no passage wide enough for his stricken body. Margo bounded up and steadied the rocking lamps.

"Kate – go after him!" Elizabeth ran back to her cousin and pulled her from the chair. "Take care of him – oh, God, it's so awful!"

On the dark stairs leading to the street Kate heard his heavy footsteps slowly going down. When she came onto the pavement, Harry was in the middle of the crowded street, waving down everything with wheels.

In the cab, his legs crashed against the door, against Kate, as they careened uptown through the late night traffic. When his knee on hers, Kate felt his heavy, cold sickness and was frightened by its intensity, then awed by his endurance. Taking a million years, he dug out his wallet and paid for the cab; another million to unzip his key chain and insert the key in the front door lock. Stricken, distant, he warned her off, warned off Mrs. Quinn, who stared aghast at his stiff, gray face.

To the women huddled in the dark hallway, he seemed to drag the walls and floor and furniture in his wake. The sound of his shoes on the bare floor was tenacious and horrifying.

Kate followed; timid, timid, entering the bedroom. She stopped dead at the sound of his vomiting. She was a silent puker but he growled and panted like a great beast.

He sat on the edge of the bed and stared at her like the king of the world while she watched as he undid his laces and pulled off his cordovans. He lay back on his elbows, watching her as she turned and took off her Jeans.

Balanced on one leg, she crashed to the rug at the sound of his soft, cracker laughter. "My God!"

He looked down at her with crafty eyes.

"You sounded crazy."

"Of course."

She stared into his sharpened, cunning face.

"What do you mean, 'of course'?"

"Of course, I sound crazy to you."

She turned away.

"You turned crazy 'cause you've been fornicatin' with your own kind."

Kate dismissed his shit with a flip hand and took a Margoesque stride toward the bathroom door.

"Yaa hoo!" He covered his mouth in mock horror. "Now, don't get upset, honey, just don't get upset, 'cause there ain't nothing that can be done about it."

"Holy crow, it's growin' right before my eyes." He pointed to her ass. He laughed wildly.

"Cut it out," she said.

"Don't ya see it? My God, girl, has your sight gone too? Don't ya see what you've got growin' back there?"

Kate reached back her hand and felt her bottom.

"Looks like a donkey tail, a long, black donkey tail that knows how to spell. Yes, it's spelling something!"

She couldn't take her eyes off his fascinated face as he slowly spelled it out. "H-I-C-K-O-R-Y, D-I-C-K-O-R-Y, D-Y-K-E. Hey, that's pretty good for a dumb, ole donkey tail."

Kate pulled on her jeans and was at the bedroom door when he called after her: "I'd tuck it inside my trousers if I were you. Never know what harm a tale-telling tail like that might do. Just coil it round that cute little ole ass of yours."

Kate closed the door on his crafty, cracker laughter, went softly into Cam's room, and climbed into her crib. A strong, roomy crib, bought by Mrs. Edwards for her granddaughter the day after she was born.

The sheet smelled pleasantly of talcum powder. Stuffing herself into every corner, Kate made a circle round her daughter, her knees nearly touching her chin.

Downtown, some white painted room would welcome them. With the income from her trust, Kate could work part time as a waitress or drive a cab, taking care of Cam during the days. She would manage and, day by day, the self-hatred that was now poisoning her would drain away.

The baby poured heat into her stomach. Slowly relaxing, Kate fell asleep.

"My father's here?" Kate lay like Gulliver under Mrs. Quinn's amused face. She tried to sit up and moaned with pain.

"Easy, now, you're all messed up." Mrs. Quinn pushed Kate's leg back through the slats and lowered the side of the crib. "I've never seen such a sight in all my life!"

Kate closed her eyes against her bright, hard voice.

"What a fright I got! Cam was walking along your back like a fence. She could have crashed down as easily as that!" Kate winced at the sharp sound of her snapping fingers. Mrs. Quinn brushed the hair out of Kate's eyes.

"You look terrible!"

"I feel terrible!" She climbed out of the crib and stood on shaking legs. "I'm getting a divorce."

"Get fixed up first," Mrs. Quinn said, patting her back. "And go in to your father, he's pacing about in there like a lion. I offered him coffee, but he didn't want any. Get going, now, I'm taking Cam out to the park."

Kate took a few steps, then stood, the sun hot on her back, sobbing.

Mrs. Quinn brushed Kate's hair with Cam's baby brush. "All right, go on and cry. I've had some rotten times with my husband, I can tell you. It passes, that's all I can say. Pull yourself together, now, we'll have a talk this afternoon."

Pacing like a lion in cinnamon tweeds with a soft green wool scarf chucked round his neck. His elegant cane clicked on the parquet floor. The gold tip flicked up at Kate as she entered the room.

Kate sat on the brown couch. Dust flying from the pillow that he molded with his cane discouraged the judge from sitting beside her. As the upholstered chair seemed distant, he stood on the other side of the coffee table, leaning on his cane.

"Where's Mother?"

His eyes bore down on her, the same color as the pale, hard sky seen in the narrow windows behind him. "Your mother isn't feeling well. In fact, she's going into the hospital tomorrow for a series of tests." His eyes lifted, moved efficiently in his skull. "I've always hated that painting. It's the purple background and the blank faces. Why does it have to be so large? But that's the style nowadays. I much prefer the one in our library."

"Is her back hurting her more?"

"It's not hurting her more but it's not hurting her less. We're scheduled to go to Europe in the spring and I want the thing cleared up by then."

"Poor Mother!"

"You modeled those figures on your mother, as I remember. The two of you sweated all summer long at the top of the house."

"You said I left the faces blank because I couldn't manage the features." Kate laughed. "You were so cheerfully insulting."

The judge smiled toughly. "I wish to God that your painter friend had the same lack of technique." The tip of his cane gleamed at her. "Where's your good husband?"

"He's in bed with the flu," Kate said protectively.

"I had dinner with Dean Bender last night. He talked at length about his female professors." A blank-faced woman reflected from the painting above existed in the shiny marble surface of the coffee table. "I was shocked at what he told me. I wanted to talk with you before I gave him any advice."

Kate wouldn't look up.

"The dean mentioned Elizabeth Graves, particularly." Kate yawned from nerves and weariness. "Did he?"

"He tells me she's a lesbian."

"Where'd he hear that?" She smiled up at her father. "Glad tidings from the birdies, or what?"

The judge looked coldly at her jeans and navy blue sweat shirt. "You dress like a toughie, Kate, but I think you're a fraud."

She stretched out her legs and admired her calloused feet. "Why, Daddy dear?"

He stepped around the coffee table and swooped down beside her on the couch. His smell assailed her and his hand, pressing hers hard, notified her of his great physical strength.

"I've stopped by on my way home especially to warn you."

The will that reduced her mother to a blithering idiot now blared at her. "Warn me of what?"

"I think it would be very foolish of you not to break off relations with Margo Schwartz."

Kate focused on the bridge of his nose as she struggled for courage. "What are you driving at?"

As his breath quickened, Kate knew that she'd hit on her defense. The hunter wished the timid deer to take fright at the sight of his gun, but she would make him fire it.

The judge got up, his cane erecting smartly as he paced. "The dean also said that Harry had taken Elizabeth under his wing. How do you feel about that?" Kate shrugged. "They're natural allies."

"Oh, come on! You get my point!"

She innocently smiled. "What is your point?" What a lark! Each question she asked was worth a year of law school. He irritably tapped the coffee table with his cane.

"Do you think I'm just a querulous old fool? Don't you understand how things work? This is not a matter to take lightly."

Kate ducked past his looming form and stood behind the upholstered chair. "It's light as air what the dean whispered into your gaping ear. Or does he have anything heavy to base it on? How did the light reach him?"

"Damn it!"

"Don't get me wrong, Dad. It's a fascinating piece of gossip, but what else is it worth?"

"Kate, your naiveté fascinates me. It's worth your husband's career." He graciously smiled. "Do you get the picture now?"

"I think it's all a bluff."

The judge looked at his watch and glared furiously at Kate. "I'm late for lunch. Your mother will be on the warpath for her drink." He strode down the hall. "I hope you see that having your name associated with that portrait will only make a bad situation much, much worse." He opened the front door. "They don't need facts, Kate." Thinking he was ringing for the elevator, Judge Edwards rang the bell of the neighboring apartment.

"They'll need them for a lawsuit."

A small boy opened the opposite door and looked gravely up at the judge. "What do you want?" Her father ignored the child and glared at Kate. "I heard what you said and you're a goddamned fool!"

"Who are you?" asked the child.

"Shut up," snapped the judge and stepped back into his daughter's apartment.

"Shut up, yourself," shouted the child, sticking out his tongue. He backed her against the door, commanding.

"There will be no lawsuit! No woman can risk that kind of publicity."

Judge Edwards rang for the elevator in three long blasts. The outraged shout of the Puerto Rican operator filled the shaft. The heavy door crashed open.

"I hear, I hear! What's the matter with you? You think I'm deaf?"

The judge ignored the bouncing little man, sent a stern look to his daughter from the car.

The operator turned round. "Think I'm deaf, hey?"

"Be quiet," said the judge.

"Me quiet? How 'bout you quiet, hey?" The door slammed shut, the little boy retired, and Kate went back to the bedroom to wake up her husband.

The huge bed was empty. Steam poured into the room through the bathroom door. Water rattled the shower curtain, dully drummed the tub.

Harry sat naked on the john, looked tragically at her through the steam. Kate buried her face in his soft, moist hair.

"I love you," she said.

"How come?"

"I'm not afraid of my father. He was just here – oh, it's so wonderful! What do you want for breakfast?" She crushed her face in his thick hair. "Oh, God, it's all so marvelous! I'll make scrambled eggs with tarragon. Hurry, I can't wait to tell you!"

Neither the eggs nor the coffee nor Kate's exultation could dispel Harry's depression. The waves of his memory slapped hard against him and he slumped at the yellow table, angry, regretful, and disbelieving.

"I slept with her right in front of you – I can't bear it."

He stuck at this point until Kate grew bored with his guilt and repeated her conversation with her father, shoving it under his nose as if it were a gun.

"They're out of their depth, Harry. It never occurred to them that Elizabeth would defend herself. They think that all they have to do is whisper the word 'lesbian' and she'll sink into the woodwork. If she accused them of blackmail, they'd back-pedal like mad."

"*I'm* out of *my* depth," he said and groaned. "I can't understand what's holding you up."

She patted his leg. "I'm telling you about this marvelous weapon my father handed me and you just sit there sweating about last night. Don't you see that you and Elizabeth can beat the shit out of them?"

He winced. "I can't stop thinking about last night. It was so modern and shallow – don't you feel that?"

"Last night I thought you were disgusting. I had no pity at all when Margo exposed you – but I see it differently now." She kissed him. "Oh, come on, lover, don't you see, they're not dealing just with homosexual women, they're dealing with us!"

Harry went to the window. Brownstone roofs stretched to the avenue. "That gay couple are working in their garden," Harry snarled. "The big, ugly one has his shirt off." He looked at her bitterly. "There's the prejudice, strong as hell. In that respect I'm a Victorian man."

"That's your Baptist past talking. That's not deep."

"I don't understand you. I slept with another woman right under your nose!" He gestured wildly. "Christ, I'd be up the wall."

"I would be screaming if you fell in love with her – "

"That old whore," he said with a sneer. "Are you crazy?"

"You're mean," she said contemptuously, "mean and unfair." He drew lines through the dirty window.

"I feel mean. I feel depraved. I feel like shit."

"Wild horses couldn't have stopped you last night."

"Because of booze and lust, which are nothing."

"You're sick because Margo's going to tell Elizabeth."

He played a methodical game of tick-tack-toe, drawing his big finger through the X's. "I hadn't thought of that. Of course, that was her aim, wasn't it – to lower me in Elizabeth's eyes." He glanced at her briefly and looked away.

"And yours."

Did his odd expression and slight faltering mean he was in love with Elizabeth? The thought hit Kate hard and she wondered, as she sat down in a panic, why it hadn't occurred to her before.

"What's really bothering you?"

"In a way, it's a relief to be toppled from her high estimation, but, Christ, not quite so far. From hero to cheap shit ain't easy on the ego. Also, I really admire Elizabeth and I hate to see that bitch hurt her."

"Oh, disgusting," Kate cried. "You should face yourself."

"You're good at that," he said bitterly. "But, then, why shouldn't you be with your high-and-mighty background? I'm a hick compared to you and I wish to hell you wouldn't have your name under that painting." He stared out the window, then glanced at her hostilely. "Now you know where I stand or don't stand, because, honey, this whole homosexuality thing is a fence I can't get over." He pushed away from the window and walked rapidly across the kitchen. His voice rang sharply in the hall. "I just can't make it."

Kate took Harry's place by the window. A church steeple, dull green and grim, reared from the sweet jumble of brownstone roofs. Straight ahead, to the left and right, luxury apartments made a valley of the old-fashioned world. Young Lochinvar came into the valley past sheer walls of pink and tan, took up residence, and prospered. For a while.

They must talk. Kate went slowly through the hall, through the living room, into the bedroom, and up to the bathroom door. She spoke softly through the crack:

"Listen, Harry." It slammed in her face. She pushed against it, then heard the lock turn.

As she made the huge bed, she strained to hear sounds behind the water that ran steadily from the tap into the sink. She piled the books on the bedside table, straightened the lampshade, dusted the mirror with her sleeve, and suddenly saw her husband framed in scrolly gold, huge in the shoulder, angelic of face; then he vanished with a flash of white buttocks. His hatred stood in the air like spears.

She sat on the bed, not daring to follow. Encouraged finally by a Bach cantata, she went timidly into the living room. "Are you really going to sit in your chair and get drunk?"

His big, naked limbs glared sullenly against the blue upholstery.

"No."

"Then, get up and get dressed."

"No," he said in the same thoughtful tone.

"What are you doing, then?"

A fierce, utterly resistant look came into his eyes,

"I'm listening to music."

"What about Mrs. Quinn? She'll be back any minute."

He smiled considerately. "Then, pass me the earphones." She did.

"Plug them in, will you?"

She did.

Harry fitted them over his ears, pulled a bottle of Scotch from behind the chair, and waved good-bye to his wife.

Dutifully, she returned his wave, got her coat from the closet, and left the apartment.

16

Kate thought that she had no desire to see Margo, thought on this mild, clear February day that the park, slightly soft underfoot and sweet-smelling in the sweep of a west wind, would be the perfect place to spend the afternoon. But she walked quickly down the slope by the sailboat pond and up the hill beyond, brushing the shoulder of a cracked rock with her own and greeting with a burst of tears the touch of pine needles as she angled her face beneath a low branch.

At the top of the old commercial building Kate knocked resentfully on the steel door, then leaned on her elbow and admired her boots. Dimly, the shriek of an ambulance carried up the long, straight stairwell and Kate found herself pounding with two fists against the door and calling out Margo's name.

The bolt slid back and as Kate came into the loft, Margo disappeared into the kitchen.

Her mean brow resting on the flank of the fridge, she glared at a pot of water on the stove, then at Kate. "Go home, the painting is finished."

"No!"

"No?" Margo grimaced. "And what does little boy blue mean by 'no'? Eh?"

Kate straddled a kitchen chair, remembered last night, and quickly changed her position.

"Why is the painting finished?"

Margo sagged against the counter. "When I woke up this morning there was no Elizabeth sleeping sweetly beside her old pal and when I made my usual paranoid check on my masterpiece, do you know what I found? Guess. No, don't. The slow shifting of your inadequate mind is more noise than I can bear." She snapped her head to the side.

"What is up with this water? It's been hours! Elizabeth took the kettle. Packed into her bag, no doubt. The witch!" She stared imperiously into cupboards. "Took the coffee too." Kate stood. "Stay where you are, don't make sudden gestures, this whole fucking kitchen is traveling at the speed of light."

Gloomily squeezing a tea bag, sucking her fingers, Margo finally answered Kate. "There'll be no more posing, sweetheart, because you're all painted up with a handlebar mustache and a pornographic cock. Elizabeth did it. Go look."

"She wouldn't have."

"*Go look!*"

In front of the portrait, looking up, looking down, Kate saw no mustache, no cock.

Behind her Margo lunged about on liquid legs, laughing like a loony teenager, collapsing as though hit on the yellow couch.

Kate looked sternly down. Margo turned onto her back, propped her head on the arm of the couch, and smiled. "You've no sense of humor, darling."

Her eyes riveted on Margo's crotch, Kate muttered: "You're stupid!"

The belt, the zipper lifted slightly and Kate threw herself on top of the painter, pressing her face against Margo's neck. Ah, she ached unbearably for this strange woman, ached for the streaks of gray on Margo's temples and the sadness in her lopsided green eyes.

"I wish I knew what made you agonize so." Margo stroked her back and bottom.

"Because I love you."

"But why is that so sad?"

"I want to die!"

Gently Margo bade Kate get up, then went to the bedroom, returning with a quilt and pillow. She stood on the red rug, beckoning with a humorous little twist of her head. "Come on over here where I can get at you."

Her lithe hip turning, Margo dug into her jeans pocket and pulled out a joint. They passed it back and forth as they undressed. Margo tossed Kate her jeans. "Put these on, I'm mad for a repeat performance."

Kate leaped joyfully at the big, luscious woman, smoke streaming from her lungs. They lay perfectly still for a long while, Kate thinking of Margo's breasts and stomach and loins until she could no longer resist her desire, then moving softly and lightly, in a moment, hammering hard.

Kate stopped and pulled off the jeans. Kneeling between Margo's legs, she whispered, "I want to feel you with me." Obligingly the painter lifted herself, tilted, maneuvered until they fitted together, then moved imperatively against Kate in a long, long race.

"Oh, God, you're really on me now! Ride me! Oh, baby, you're beautiful, beautiful!"

Difficult, this riding. The contact was elusive but Kate remembered Margo's tremendous effort with Harry and she kept going, raising excited sounds from Margo and a fine moisture that covered her body like dew.

"Divine," Margo shouted. "Oh, stay! Stay, just a moment more."

The longest, lowest sound from deep in her chest pealed out from the painter, plaintive, urgent, and piercing. Kate's stomach vibrated with it, then tingled exquisitely as though woken from a deep sleep. Kate put her hand there and knelt over Margo in amazement.

"Do you make love like that all the time?" she asked.

The painter opened one eye. "Never so intensely. Nope, never. That was something."

Kate threw back her head and whistled triumphantly.

"Did you make it?" Margo asked.

"No."

"Stubborn woman – you were certainly excited enough."

"Oh, my, my, my! Land sakes, lady, ain't never been so happy in my whole life. If my back weren't broken and my legs turned to stone, I'd try that again."

Margo looked at her fondly. "You're a born womanizer. I haven't met a chick with such zest in all my days."

The term "womanizer" shot Kate down. She crawled under the quilt and lay apart from Margo, feeling cold and unspeakably vulgar. Womanizing had nothing to do with liberation. It was the pathetic aping of the warrior male. Oh, dreadful to buzz below decks like a hive of bees in service of a fantasy so fawning and sick. Feeling Margo's amused gaze, Kate pulled the quilt over her head to hide her violent blush.

"Funny, dear Kate Stevens, what's the matter?"

"I'm a male chauvinist pig," Kate moaned through the material. "I'm a parody of a male chauvinist pig. I should be shot!" Margo kissed her hooded head. "Then, be it, darling. Get as deep into it as you can, go every inch of the way, and respect yourself on the journey. OK?"

Kate threw back the quilt. "It's so obscene to want to be a huge man!"

"You don't come on to me that way at all."

How did Kate come on, then? How queer that she'd never thought to ask.

"You've a lot of force, a terrific amount which is just starting outward. It's natural to want to bang away – you saw me with your husband – it's natural to want to play every part and you feel obscene because you've been taught in so many various and subtle ways that to take and move and get is for men only."

"You called me a phony boy." Margo kissed Kate lightly on the mouth.

"You are boyish but you're also girlish and very womanly. You're an incredibly charming combination of he and she and mother and child and it's high time you realized it." She softly belched.

"Elizabeth tramps the streets and calls for action but really the only thing a woman must do these days is respect herself." She pinched Kate's cheek. "That's truly revolutionary."

Kate played with Margo's breasts as if they were water, scooping up their cool weight and softness and letting them overflow her cupped hands. A sudden rush of joy made her laugh.

"I was ice until I met you."

Margo lay back on her arm. "Elizabeth said that to me many times, but she fights it so!"

"She's jealous of where you are. I was jealous of Harry. It's a horrible feeling."

"Jealous of him?" Margo sneered.

"I was the Snow Queen, remember?"

"You could be dead and still be in no hurry to catch up to that moron." She put her hand over Kate's mouth and shrugged. "I used to be a mute."

"You? I don't believe it."

"I shut up the year my father died. He was my ally in a ferociously embattled household. It was me and my father against brother Bill and my mother and when syphilis removed my daddy from the scene – yes, syphilis, that's something, isn't it? It was a nice, respectable, prosperous family and the doctors kept thinking that the symptoms must mean something else until there was no mistaking it. My nice, sympathetic daddy had gone out and gotten himself a social disease. He died very slowly, going nuts as he did so."

"I don't know why I decided for silence. It was grief and also protest. My mother and brother hated my father for disgracing them. Their self-pity was appalling and they worked out a little act that moved them no end. My mother would lie quietly on her bed, for days sometimes, then rustle into the kitchen, turn on the gas, and stick her head in the oven. Her pathetic coughing, louder by the moment, would finally alert brother Bill

231

and he'd rush from the television set and haul her out. They'd sob together in the kitchen and look at me hatefully if I dared to come in." Margo snapped her fingers and laughed.

"A fantastic team!"

"The day after the anniversary of my father's death was my birthday. I was eighteen and thought I deserved a lift. I went out and bought fifty pairs of spectator shoes – remember them? White and brown and awful-looking? I spent the whole day in shoe salons, charging and sending on mother's account. The doorbell never stopped ringing for a day, nor did the banging of the oven door. All those boxes of identical sizes just coming and coming. Horror of horrors! What would the maid, the doorman, and the neighbors think?"

Margo laughed ruefully. "To the stove! Wait, wait, save your tears, the sad part comes later. The old lady really turned on me. She'd had enough eccentricity, enough social exposure. She convinced her pet shrink that I was as crazy as my father when he died, that nursing him had unhinged me, and with the permission of my brother, who was now, you understand, the head of the household, she had me committed to the state egg box."

Margo brooded. "I never blamed my mother because she was so gone. I think she was born gone. But brother Bill hated me because of my relationship with Dad and he deliberately bitched me up. He took advantage of the silent stuff, you see, and moved me right out. So did the fucking doctors. They said I was a schizophrenic (the disease of the day, you understand) and gave me insulin shots, which made me as fat as my mother. That was the worst – Jesus, that was agony! My body was the only comfort I had and they turned it into a pile of fat!"

Margo touched Kate's wet eyes and meditatively sucked her fingers. "Delicious tears, my darling. It's so sweet to be cried over. I just love you for it and love me better when I remember how miserable I was. Looking back, I can see how angry I must have been. Refusing to talk was a weapon, horribly ineffective, because my mother had no trouble with that – just turned me into a pile of fat, locked me in a room, and gave the key to the state."

She took Kate's hand. "Here's the reason I'm telling you all this. One morning when the needle man came calling, I started to scream. I screamed that I'd been framed, that I was perfectly sane, that I wanted out. I screamed tirelessly until they put me under with a shot. It was like being ducked-up I'd bob, loud in the mouth, then" – her big finger jabbed her arm – "down I'd go. Went on for days. The long and short of it, my sweet crybaby, is that I got out and I've been screaming ever since."

Margo drew Kate down and casually stroked her breast. "The only point of that story is to show you that one must fight. It makes no difference where one starts from or where one ends because the value is all in the struggle." Kate's scalp tingled at Margo's touch. "But, you've begun. You're on your way and let me tell you something. Before your operation" – her fingers glided along the scar, plucked at the flat nipple – "before your misfortune, you were just the kind of gal my mother would approve of, which is death, you know, insidious, living death."

Her hand closed tightly over Kate's breast and she said gruffly: "Now you're someone that I approve of, and that, sweetheart, is the best compliment you ever got in your life."

"I love you," Kate shouted. "I do, do, do!" Lightly and playfully, Margo kissed Kate's mouth, face, and hands. "Love yourself. It's the answer."

The phone rang. Kate threw her arms around Margo's shoulders and hung on for dear life.

"I'm going to answer, my dear, but remember this. If you can love me you can love yourself." She kissed Kate's forehead. "Now, let go."

"No!" Kate held grimly.

"Let go!"

Kate lay under the quilt and watched Margo take up the phone, the white curly cord stretching straight as she pulled it into the hall.

Walking back into the room, Margo went among her painting lights, flicking them on. Morbidly absorbed in Margo's sprightly feet, Kate climbed onto the platform.

"Oh, hell, I'm so distracted. That was Elizabeth on the phone. She's heard a rumor that she'd been censured at the faculty meeting. She also said that she called your distinguished husband for verification and advice and that he was at home, dead, raving drunk."

"Poor Harry," Kate said at last, feeling unspeakably sad.

"That moron." Margo sneered. Kate looked away from her coarse, cruel expression, no different from the one Harry had shown when he'd called Margo an old whore. Yet Margo was up on her feet and painting as usual while Harry was drunk in his chair.

"He's gone to pieces," Kate said softly. "It's horrible."

"Forget that, kiddo, he's just showing what he is."

"No, Margo, he's really flipped out. This morning he said he wished I wouldn't have my name under the painting and that homosexuality was too much for him. Then he locked himself in the bathroom. When I left the apartment, he was sitting naked in the living room, listening to music with the earphones on, as if" – Kate began to cry – "as if he were invisible." Margo stared viciously up at her.

"Stop that crying at once."

Kate could not and Margo took her by the arm and pulled her roughly down the steps. "I don't need you to finish this painting, you stupid girl! It's a matter of toenails – oh, God, stop that damned crying."

Kate walked blindly to the rug and collected her clothes, going back to the platform to put them on. Margo followed her, shouting.

"It's incredible to me, absolutely incredible, that you've failed to realize that posing for this painting is the most important thing you've ever done. To have your name under it is an honor, because it's not just you I've been putting down but an important, original, beautiful idea. Your little face and figure are standing in for something great, my darling, and don't you ever forget it."

Unbuttoned, unzipped, Kate stood trembling. "Fuck your idea," she mumbled.

Margo grabbed her. "What?"

"Fuck your fucking idea, fuck face! Harry's a person and he's suffering!"

Margo thrust her chin forward and pulled at her hair

235

in a preposterous expression of rage. "If I ever see you again – if I ever see you after you've been with that slimy, disgusting, careerist creep, I'll kill you!"

Margo lunged, her hand raised. But in mid swing the painter let out a womanly wail and crumpled to the floor as Kate struck first. The young woman then sat down on the platform and pulled on her boots. Went down like a pack of cards, she thought, and grinned into Margo's outraged, extravagant eyes. The painter sat hunched and cross-legged, feeling her mouth with intense solicitude.

"Is it swollen?" She moaned.

Kate knelt and took away Margo's hand. She looked seriously into Margo's prideless, vain eyes. "A tiny bit."

"Oh, God, if it's swollen for the opening, I'll die."

Kate opened the heavy steel door, then turned and watched the painter proceed to the bathroom with tiny, crisis-laden steps. "If you need a dentist," she called, "I've got a good one."

A high, wild wail was her answer and Kate, softly closing the door, flew down shallow steps as though bursting from a funnel of hard, persistent purpose. Running on the lighted pavements, humming under the subway's boom, she felt ecstatically vulnerable in all her senses and momentarily new.

The night elevator man was asleep on the leather couch, his teeth irritably showing in his flung-back head. Kate walked the five flights to her floor, then lingered in the dim hall. The ticks and creaks of the walls and the humming light above her head welcomed her from the sharp, windy night. Its ocean of low sound was heard even in the core of this thick, respectable building – spurting sharply from time to time, a bark, a horn, a shout.

Margo's outburst possessed her mind. Her hand, flying against Margo's face, was the gesture of a person that Kate had not realized she'd become. She pressed back against the front door as Harry came down the narrow hall. In the dim light his white T-shirt and shorts loomed ominously.

"What are you doing home?" he coldly asked.

She followed him into the kitchen, the fridge door flashing at her, barring her passage, as Harry got out the ice. She watched him get down only one glass from the cupboard and while he poured his drink she stood timidly beside him, stretching for the high shelf. She felt Harry's breath on her head and his leg against hers as he swiftly reached down another glass.

"You're very small for a red-hot lover."

"Balzac was only five foot two, with short legs and a huge stomach." She smiled falsely. "He was wildly successful with women."

"Shut up, you bitch!" His arms swept out and bore her up over his head, an outraged howl streaming up into her face. Then he perched her on top of the fridge, got his drink, hauled out a chair for his feet, and lolled at the yellow table, regarding her with humorous eyes.

"If you can climb up a box, you can climb down one."

"I can't."

His brow arched flirtatiously. "Can't?"

"Ever since Cam and her big head, I wet my pants every time I jump."

"A likely story, miss," he said in a stern voice.

"It's very embarrassing."

"Prove it!"

She jumped. Harry reached forward and put his hand between her legs.

"My god! You're as wet as Cam!"

In the bathroom Kate took off her boots and jeans, washed out her underpants, and took a quick shower. Dressed in one of Harry's skivvy shirts, she pushed open the door, the yellow bathroom light flowing over the rug and up the side of the bed. Kate followed it, shyly lifting the covers and slipping in beside her husband.

"I put your drink on the table." She grabbed his pointing hand and squeezed it hard.

"You looked so cute on top of the fridge, like a child." He turned his head suddenly, his sad, pensive eyes directed to the bureau. "Elizabeth is cute, too. She's so big and solid to be cute, but she is. A big, sweet, gallant child. She went through one hell of a battle today, as you probably heard."

"I haven't seen Elizabeth," Kate said dismally. She yearned to be told that she was gallant too.

He laughed wanly. "She's probably getting up another petition." He drank for a while, then burst out: "That wily, clever, vindictive fuck. He enjoyed it so!" The clap of his hands was like a gunshot. "He reveled!"

"Who?"

"He kept looking at me to be sure I knew I was getting it back. I had him good that day at his club, but he got me today!" He sighed and bit his lip. "Shit!"

"Are you talking about Dean Bender?"

"These old, rich conservatives are so clever. He had Elizabeth from beginning to end because he's such a wily pie. She wanted to argue the merits of the thing, liberals

238

always do, but he just fobbed her off. He was so reasonable, so charming and indirect. Elizabeth kept challenging him to discuss the substance of her position but he stuck to arguing the procedure. At the end of an hour he had the entire faculty eating out of the palm of his hand."

"Is this to do with Elizabeth's petition?"

"The feeling is very strong against her. The worst enemy a faculty has is its students and Elizabeth broke ranks. But still the old fart played his cards so that there wasn't a chance of her arousing sympathy, and, by God, there's a potentially strong sentiment against the curriculum committee, especially among the younger faculty. "Ain't that something?" He whistled softly.

"Listen, I realize that Elizabeth and Dean Bender had it out, but where?"

"Dean Bender called a special faculty meeting this afternoon, to get our blessing, as he expressed it in his chatty way, to get our blessing for his proposal that it be made clear to Miss Graves that either she appeal through normal channels and abide by the decision of the properly constituted authority or she look for another job."

"The properly constituted authority," Kate cried. "That's a matter of opinion."

"You sound exactly like Elizabeth. She did her damnedest to persuade us that, if the questions she'd raised were right, it was ridiculous to censor her, or unorthodox procedure."

"You mean she was appealing right there at the faculty meeting? That's exciting!"

"It was hopeless. Elizabeth would demand to know whether the law school was being run for the convenience

239

of the curriculum committee or if the interests of the students were its primary concern

The dean would cross his legs or light his pipe or, best, he'd rub his eyes and make it appear that he, a judicious, clear-sighted man, was being bullied and kept from his duties by an ignorant woman with painful manners. He kept saying that he had no intention of wasting his colleagues' time with whether or not a certain course should be dropped or reinstated. That was the domain of the curriculum committee and the reason why it had been created was precisely to relieve the faculty of such routine administrative work.

"He said that Miss Graves could call the committee a cabal of reactionary old men if she liked, but they were doing their colleagues a great service by planning and regulating a large and varied curriculum. It was difficult enough to get his brilliant professors together as often as was necessary but if their attendance were required every time a decision on the curriculum was questioned, why, he'd have no faculty left in the school. Didn't the prima donnas love that! Shit!"

Then your cousin interrupted the dean – causing scowls and mutters – to ask if he didn't think it was unfair to the students to have a course taught by an instructor with no qualifications," – Harry held up his hand – "then the dean interrupted her to say that he agreed that her lack of qualifications was a serious problem but one that he preferred to take up with her personally."

"Ow, ow, ow!"

He pressed her shoulder. "Then, while he had them all laughing, he called for a voice vote. Did he have their blessing or did he not? He did, so overwhelmingly that he didn't even call for the nays."

"What did you do?" she asked sympathetically.

"I sat on my ass." He bitterly laughed. "Every time the dean directed a sarcastic smile in my direction, I smiled pleasantly back." He got up and looked into the long, door mirror. "I smiled like this." He turned and shot her a bland, blind smile.

"Did Elizabeth look at you?"

"Yup, she did." He turned back to the mirror and arranged his face. "I looked as stout and loyal as I could, so that she could take courage, don't you know."

"Well?" Kate waited for him to turn and show her his expression.

"That's it – the back of my head!" He put one hand on his hip and gestured to himself with the other.

"'Harry boy, you have given that grundy old dean the satisfaction of knowing that you are the right man for the job. He's seen you detach yourself with an admirable maturity from people whose politics might be embarrassing for a man in a responsible position. He's witnessed great development of self-control and objectivity in his handpicked successor. When he came up to you after the meeting, he knew that the judiciousness of his advice would not be lost on such a tough-minded, self-sacrificing person as yourself. When he said to you: 'That damned lesbian isn't worth it, son,' he knew that you wouldn't be insulted, that he could pat your back in his contemptuous way and you'd go right on pleasantly smiling."

He rapped his knuckles on the glass, a light, rapid

drumroll, then lay quietly down on the bed. "When your dad called a few hours ago, I was so panicked that I didn't even feel the next half bottle of Scotch." He sucked in his cheeks and gave her a quick, wretched look. "I tell you, Katey, these have not been my finest hours. Your father – "

She put her hand over his mouth. "My father told you that no man stands a chance in academic circles if his wife is rumored to be a lesbian. Bah!"

He sank back on the bed. "I can't help it, Katey, the whole thing scares the shit out of me."

She turned and leaned over him. "Well, it is terribly scary, but not in the way my father paints it. He'd like to think he's so important that there will be a column in the Times' social page about Judge Edwards' scandalous lesbian daughter. He also likes to think that nothing has changed since they put Oscar Wilde in jail." She kissed his cheek. "But that's his mind, not yours."

He ruefully laughed. "I'm down, you're up."

"I got news for you, hon! Come the morrow, we'll both be up!" Grinning, she stretched her arms above her head. "Up, up, and away!"

"Wonder Woman," he muttered and turned his head. "What's the matter?"

"You've been nosing round that cunt!"

She sat cross-legged and said with mock formality: "I don't think you should refer to my friend as a cunt."

"She's not your friend – her cunt aside. She's your enemy."

"I know," she said softly. "Such hatred!" She threw her leg over Harry and sat lightly on his stomach.

"I've killed sharks in the ocean's depth, gleaming

panthers have dropped at my feet. I've seen Margo stoned to death and rise up, hung with paint pots and her teeth full of brushes. I've seen my husband making love" – she winked – "in the name of equal rights, of course, and I'm here to tell you, sprung from guilt, delivered from dread, that all is well!" She dived down beside him. "I've got so many things to tell you. It's so exciting, Harry! I've been so frightened all my life and now I'm not."

She crawled up his side. "Want to fuck? Oh, God, you're blushing!"

He turned his face. "You're talking like Margo."

"I'm sorry!" She looked down at him and suddenly found his red face silly. "No, I'm not sorry! Why should I be sorry? Margo's a fighter – just wait until you hear – but we've got to go to sleep because the opening's tomorrow." She leaned across him and turned off the light. "Don't worry, don't fret – we're a team; right?"

He turned away from her and curled up on his side. Kate poked him. "Right?"

"I'm thinking that I want to have my coronation dream one last time."

"The one where you were crowned dean of the law school?"

He laughed softly. "One last time!"

Kate pressed up against his back. "Go to sleep and I'll whisper the details into your ear." She waited until Harry's breathing was deep and regular. "Once upon a time, on a cold, bright autumn day, in a gray town, filled with gray men, there was this coat rack – "

"Stinker," Harry whispered. "Can't trust you."

"There was going to be a procession from the church

243

to the town square. Flags were hung out along the way and the streets were swept and washed for the first time in years. The Royal Scots Guards had been hired for the day and the Boston Symphony Orchestra was setting up in the nave of the cathedral. All the sweet, blond children under three were mad to get into their wings and do the number they'd been practicing for months – "

"Bitch," Harry managed, then gently began to snore.

Curved lightly against his back, Kate lay in the rhythm of his breathing as though in the sea. Face down, she floated with ease, happy at the thought of Cam existing in the next room, of Margo living, a foot or hand flung out to touch Elizabeth.

Yet beneath them all, drug-weighted, her mother was a relentless traveler, each night sounding deeper until her husband's voice was a tiresome echo in her ear.

"Do you love me? Mary, Mary, do you love me?"

She was so cramped, so terribly tired. Oh, what did he want? Love me! His need hooking her, reeling her back, she woke to read his panic at the places she'd been.

17

The yearly show of American Contemporary Artists was held in a recently constructed building across the street from the park. It was an impressive but playful structure, surrounded by a dry moat and entered by a ramp.

On the night of the opening, when Margo's painting was finally to be seen, Kate and Harry ate a sandwich and had a drink before leaving the apartment. Kate had brushed her black sweater, sewed a button on her tweed jacket, and pressed her jeans in an effort to look as neat as she could in her favorite costume.

The young woman had thought herself perfectly calm until she heard herself shout at Mrs. Quinn for suggesting she wear one of her "lovely" dresses. In his dark English suit and wide tie, Harry lay back on the chaise with his drink and watched her dress.

"People will think I'm your sugar daddy," he said, then cringed at her irritation.

The wind was at their back as they walked west to the museum; the funnel of dark, narrow streets gave it a mournful sound that dropped away as they turned onto the broad avenue. They walked past a line of taxis and limousines waiting to let their passengers off at the ramp.

Kate looked for her parents in the steady stream of people passing into the museum. In the moat below the ramp, the gestures of the statues were blithely sardonic. As they passed into the building, a gigantic red flag cracked out pistol sounds in the strong night wind.

The lobby was jammed. Harry and Kate held hands as they edged across the marble floor to the elevator. Harry pointed out the gigantic proportions of the steel doors, while Kate, sure that the slow movement of this young and cheerful crowd would infuriate her parents, kept looking around for them. She looked especially hard at the coat-check line, for the imposition of having to check their things, whether they would or no, could well send them bitching back down the ramp and into the judge's limousine, in which they'd fume on the drive home at their daughter's eccentricities and the barbarities of modern life.

The enormous steel doors slowly opened. A uniformed black man, made tiny by the vast box behind him and the midnight blue interior that stretched above his head, quietly said: "Let them off, please."

Kate felt Harry stiffen. He said softly: "There's Elizabeth." She peered into the crowd pushing off the elevator.

Harry turned her head to the window.

"No, there – coming up the ramp."

Queened by the long ramp, the crackling flag, Elizabeth swung along in her stylish boots and raincoat. Inside the building, walking through, she observed the crowd with a calm, amused eye.

Taking Kate's arm, holding out her hand to Harry, Elizabeth pushed to the back of the elevator. Her eyes traveled up and up. "Enormous," she murmured, "Margo's painting could be stood on itself three times."

She squeezed Kate's hand. "You won't believe it when the doors open. You're hanging directly in front of the elevator. Trust Margo to get the most strategic spot." She spread her hands. "The doors slowly part and ta ta, Kate Stevens! The effect's terrific!" She spoke laughingly to Harry. "When the doors are closed you can see the entire painting reflected in the steel. Margo took me up yesterday, laughing up her sleeve because she gets 'em coming and going. The old cynic.

"It's beautiful, though," she hurried to say, "the best thing she's done. A lot of her painter pals have said that she's revived their interest in the Dutch School, which to me is a bunch of asparagus. God, people are so educated and so stupid."

The elevator slowed. Her cool eyes resting on Harry's profile, Elizabeth teased: "It's not a hanging, you know." He smiled and put his arm around her shoulders. "It's a grand opening!"

As the doors opened, Harry cupped his mouth.

"Ta, ta!"

In a fit of embarrassment, Kate hit his chest hard. "It's nice." He coughed.

Kate looked once through the parting doors, the huge figure bounding into her consciousness. Flanked by Harry and Elizabeth, she went a few steps, then ducked behind a pillar as they greeted Margo. She stared at her sleeve, counted the colors in the weave, and waited for the beating of her heart to slow. From the back of the elevator, looking past an ancient ear, a swirl of white hair, Kate had seen what she had sometimes seen in a store window or the fender of a car, her face a beautiful image flashing into her unguarded consciousness. Margo had proclaimed her essence. The fact of its existence blazed like the sun through Kate's disturbed inner view of herself as she crouched behind the pillar. There was no escaping it, the young woman saw that she was lovely.

"Well, where is she?" Margo demanded.

Unsentimental, brash, vain, childish, and harshly egotistical. Hadn't Kate grown tired of the woman, hadn't she batted her across the mouth and gone home blissfully to her own bed?

"She's hiding behind the pillar, for God's sake!"

The ironic, humorous voice, the spicy perfume invaded her nostrils. Dry in the mouth, wet in the crotch, she kissed Margo's faintly swollen lips and clutched her handsome shoulders.

"You don't have to hide there: People are saying very nice things about the big you. You should be proud."

"I am, Margo! When I saw it from the elevator – "

Kate faltered.

"I know." Margo excitedly smiled. "I had no idea the thing had come together so. When those elevator doors open – it's terrific!"

They stood close together. Margo caustically looked her over. "Your dress jeans, I presume?"

Kate admired Margo's black velvet suit. "You look marvelous. That's a nice ruffled shirt – it's not too much."

"Exactly, darling! It's taken me years to hit upon the

not-too-much ruffle. Life is so valuable in that way, these small, vital discoveries just inching along. One can't speed the pace, to try is just to muck it up. Look!" Her big, bony wrist encased in not-too-much ruffle shot past Kate's nose.

"See that little bowl of acid who just walked up? That brown three-piece-suit job? That's Harry Jones, the critic. The critic, baby!" Margo pushed out her pelvis, then her chin. "He's thinking that his mother had her left breast removed and that's exactly the way it looked."

The critic stepped close to the painting and bent. "Oh, oh, the sharp little shit has discovered the toenails. A ruinous review is coming clear in his mind. A bitter day, he's thinking, when the realists aren't real."

Her hands flashed pewter as they arranged to a more ominous position the broad brim of her black Spanish hat. One hand on her hip, the elbow grazing Kate's side, Margo turned gracefully at the sound of her name.

"See you in a while." She sauntered toward the elevator. "I think Elizabeth and Harry husband are at the bar. Did you know that there is actually a law school in Anchorage?"

Bright, exotic people swept through the steel doors. Margo rocked in the flow, laughing, calling out name after name.

Head down, moving away, Kate heard a low, urgent voice calling her name. Her mother's voice. Kate peered into the group that slowly moved out of the elevator, so slowly that Mrs. Edwards, when Kate finally saw her, had not been able to step beyond the doors and was now, her arms feebly protesting, being pushed back and back by another crowd getting on.

Kate rushed to the elevator and strained for her mother's hand, lightly grasping the fingers before they were borne out of reach.

"Clear the doors, please," the elevator man said quietly. Kate stood in the track of the closing doors, her arm flung out.

"Watch out," cried a woman. Kate leaped back, the thick, soft rubber edges closing on her wrist. The reflection of the huge face of the portrait appeared, just as Elizabeth described. Then the doors parted and quickly came together again as Kate pulled back her hand. In the momentary gap her mother's eyes, magnified in the pools of her glasses, fixed on her in terror.

"Shit," Kate cried, hearing her voice from a distance, as though she were another person. "What shall I do now?"

Take the stairs, yes, the stairs and there was the exit door to the right of the elevator. Hard, sharp-edged marble stairs that rattled her frame. "My God," cried a tiny, frightened voice in her head, "oh, my God!"

Her mother was not in the lobby. The gleaming steel doors were shut. Kate clattered back up the stairs, her hands fast hauling on the bright, cold wood railing.

Ah, Christ! The heavy exit door slamming behind her, Kate saw her mother, saw Margo taking her arm in the swirling crowd. Coming close, coming in from the side, Kate noticed the bones in her mother's face, grown sharper than her eyes.

Mrs. Edwards turned her face for Kate to kiss. "Be gentle," she murmured, then glanced at Margo. "I'm so glad to have met your friend." She looked at the painting for a long while, her blurred, troubled eyes blinking rapidly. She put her hand on Margo's arm and turned to her.

"You've certainly caught that expression. I'm delighted."

Margo bowed. "I'm so sorry to hear about your back. Two years ago I had this nagging, awful pain, right here." She turned and touched the base of her spine. "It really slowed me up. I could paint for only an hour at a time."

"Really?" Mrs. Edwards brightened. "Did you have it looked at?"

"I went through every test there was! I spent one entire winter in damp hospital basements, waiting my turn."

Mrs. Edwards smiled. "Isn't it hell? Hours and hours in those drafty halls, no light to read by, just waiting."

"And most of the doctors are so cold and arrogant they make you think you're a criminal."

"Oh, God, yes! They make you think you're making it all up. But who would make up such a dreadful pain? They must be insane!"

"My brother's a doctor, never wanted to be anything else, and I know he's a sadist." Mrs. Edwards looked almost gay. "But you got through it?"

"The pain went away in the summer. Couldn't you get off to some warm place and just bake in the sun?"

"Don't go to Europe, Mother! Take two weeks in Jamaica."

Mrs. Edwards took Kate's hand and turned to the elevator. As Margo walked along beside her, she put her hand through the painter's arm.

"You girls are wonderful! You've really cheered me up."

As she walked, she trailed her right leg. At each step her foot came almost out of her shoe. The slow, dragging sound on the brisk marble, the way her mother tottered over the threshold of the elevator, filled Kate with dread.

Downstairs, across the lobby, the dragging sound continued as Mrs. Edwards walked toward the ramp, Margo touched her shoulder. "But you must have had a coat."

Searching, sighing, her thin fingers pressed white on the gold rim of her purse, Mrs. Edwards grew paler by the moment and moved agitatedly from foot to foot. Kate took the big purse and ignored the complaints at her back as she pushed into the coat-check line. Frantically, she searched every slit of her mother's wallet, every crevice of her purse, and found finally the pink square of cardboard deep down the throat of an ancient glasses case.

Margo took the purse while Kate slipped the fur coat over her mother's arms and shoulders, smoothing the bright, soft hair behind the collar.

Mrs. Edwards responded to Margo's praise for the coat. "It may be mink, my dear, but it's been in the family for forty years. It was my mother's and her last words to me as she lay dying in that ghastly hospital were to get the coat out of the house before the appraisers came."

Kate walked her mother down the ramp. "I hope you're not upset about your father's not coming."

"Not at all."

They went slowly. The arm Kate held was shockingly frail. "He thinks you're outrageous at the moment, but

252

never forget that he loves you very much!"

They came to the curb.

"Oh, God, where's the car?"

At the end of the row a black car pulled out and swooped down.

"Here, Mother," Kate cried out, holding the door. The gigantic red flag snapped viciously in the wind. Dragging her foot, Mrs. Edwards came across the sidewalk. Struggling into the backseat, she left her shoe, which tottered and fell on its side on the pavement. Kate picked it up, then held open the car door against her mother's feeble pull. She passed the shoe in.

"Let me kiss you!"

Mrs. Edwards looked up, annoyed. "Gently, please."

Kate kissed her mother's gray cheek and bowed her head for a moment on her shoulder.

"You're a good daughter," she said.

The door slammed. The black car flew.

"Kate," Margo yelled. "Where are you going?"

She ran down the ramp, her hands flapping, her feet turned out. In Kate's old school they would have laughed at her for running like a girl.

"Don't you know that you're supposed to run on your toes?"

"Well, I've never run after anyone in my life," Margo panted. "Are you all right?"

"No!"

"Are you going to cry?"

"Yes!"

"Crybaby!"

"I know." Kate walked to the curb.

"Cry in the lighted streets," Margo called. "Don't you dare go into the park."

Kate focused on the thick stone park wall and the stolid, determined sound of her heels on the pavement. One wept in dark places, in closets, under beds, and in nighttime parks. Cry in the lighted streets, Margo had advised. Kate swerved at the heavy gates and went on down the bright sidewalk under a roof of brown leaves that clicked and rattled in the wind.

Looking so dark and sinister in her broad-brimmed hat, her ruffles fluttering in the wind, Margo had tossed out a magical phrase, a leavening phrase, and with every step Kate took, she felt its buoyancy spread through her consciousness, through her grieving flesh, and into her bones. Her feet lightly tapped the pavements and, seeing Margo's dark form walking back up the ramp, Kate quietly laughed and turned back to the museum.

If you wish to be remembered, you must write your name upon a stone and cast it deep within the sea.

In the deep-sea bottom of Kate's feeling the statue stood. Some days, when swimming, the waters were so clear it seemed she might stretch out an arm and touch the Grecian nose, the stately hands. The sorrowing face beckoned beneath the empty swing of her arm. But she'd grown to love the bright, warm water and would no longer dive into the cold. Seeing her own hands flash in the waves, she gaily followed them.

About the Author

Joan Hawkins was born in Cambridge, Massachusetts. She attended Bennington College and New York University. She lived most of her life in Manhattan, where she practised psychotherapy.

Her debut novel, *Underwater*, was published by GP Putnam in 1974. The book was critically acclaimed, challenging traditional gender roles and exploring controversial issues of the day. The second edition of *Underwater* was published on its fortieth anniversary by Landon Books in 2014.

The author's second novel, *Bailey* (2012), explores themes of addiction and childhood trauma. *Trespass* (2013), is a fascinating portrait of a moribund, spirited woman living joyously to the end. Her fourth work, *Rematch* (2021), set in the early eighties, is a prescient take on corporate sexual discrimination. Joan's fifth title the political drama, *Family Money*, along with the electronic edition of *Underwater*, was published by 451 Editions in 2022.

For more, see: www.joanhawkins.net

Landon Books

Made in the USA
Columbia, SC
09 August 2022

64901910R10157